THE LOVING TOUCH

BOOK THREE OF THE TOUCH SERIES

STONI ALEXANDER

SILVERSTONE PUBLISHING

Published in the U.S. by SilverStone Publishing, 2018
ISBN 978-1-946534-04-0 (Print Paperback)
ISBN 978-1-946534-05-7 (Kindle eBook)

To author Magda Alexander

*Thank you for making such a positive difference
in my writing...and in my life.*

I am forever grateful.

JAGGER'S RETURN

S JAGGER LOVING READ the online article, now trending on social media, his blood boiled.

Jagger Loving, CEO of Loving Resorts, better known as "God's gift to the hospitality industry", is slated to open his fourth Loving Resort. And this time we're the lucky ones because this luxurious and all-inclusive property is located on his home turf, the good 'ole USA.

Couples who crave the exotic and the erotic are flocking to the grand opening of Loving Malibu, located in—you guessed it—picturesque Malibu, California. But something is off and the rumor mill is aflutter. The "sexy-sexy" that has made Loving both rich and famous...or maybe we should say infamous...is missing. Has the handsome playboy lost his pizazz? Did that bump in the road stop him dead in his tracks? Has the hospitality mogul gone soft?

The resort's grand opening is slated for Valentine's Day. And ladies, for those of you who can't get enough of Loving, here's a recent shot of Jagger buying a bum breakfast. Don't you wish you were *that* guy?

He glared at the accompanying photo. How the hell had the paparazzi found him at that ungodly hour? He'd been in the nation's capital for two damned days and he couldn't even buy a man breakfast without someone plastering his business all over the Internet. When Jagger had lived at his Switzerland and Bora Bora properties, no one had tracked his every move. He wasn't hounded at Loving Mexico, either, until the incident that made him front-page news.

Shifting on the stool, he surveyed the Georgetown coffee shop. Nobody paid him any attention. Nowadays, he liked flying well below the radar. More than the unwanted publicity, he detested when others referred to the homeless as bums. He'd been homeless and he was no bum.

His phone rang with the ringtone for his assistant, Robby Sutton. "Morning," he answered.

"Jagger, I couldn't get the photo retracted," Robby blurted. "Upside is that you were doing something charitable. Where are you, by the way?"

"Across the street, blending in at the coffee shop." Jagger glanced outside at the pedestrians scurrying by in heavy winter coats. "Are you in your suite?"

"Yes. The car service will be here in five. I'll meet you outside the hotel. And everything is confirmed for your soiree tonight."

During his assistant's pregnant pause, Jagger shifted the phone to his other ear and waited. Robby's silence was never a good sign.

"Have you heard from Erin?" Robby asked, his voice tight.

Of all his event directors, she'd been the least communicative. "No. Should I expect a call from her?"

"She hasn't shown up for work in three days."

Ah, hell. "Has anyone contacted her?" Jagger asked as an attractive woman slipped onto the stool beside him.

"I sent her a text and left her a message. Rumor amongst the staff is that she walked. We open in one week and she's MIA." The urgency in his assistant's voice wasn't helping.

Jagger lowered his voice. "I can't leave until I cast my vote at the conference this afternoon. Fly back and find out what's going on."

"Got it."

"Keep me posted." Jagger ended the call. Last minute emergencies were to be expected, but he couldn't afford a missing event director. So much hinged on the breadth of activities offered at a Loving Resort.

"Good morning." The woman seated next to him shot him a cool smile. "Welcome back to America, Mr. Loving. I see you're flying solo. Is everything business as usual now that things have *quieted down?*"

Jagger's guts roiled, but he shot her a wink, slung his computer bag over his shoulder, and rolled out. He could not get a break from the damned media. An entire year had passed since the debacle. Why hadn't the journalists moved on? *Must be a slow day in DC politics.*

After crossing the street and sliding into the waiting sedan, Jagger muttered hello.

"Same location as yesterday, sir?" asked the chauffeur.

"Yes." As the car pulled away from the curb, Jagger's phone rang again. "Good morning, Kate."

A year ago, he'd hired Kate Faraday to help him manage through the incident at Loving Mexico. She had done a fantastic job, so he retained her services.

"I didn't like the article." He could hear the frustration in his publicist's voice. "Did you know that photographer was there?"

It wasn't even eight o'clock in the morning and he was already plum out of patience. "Kate, I bought a man breakfast. Period. When are you flying to Malibu?"

"Over the weekend," she replied. "I've set up media day for Monday. Get a haircut or use gel. You look like a wild man."

On a grunt, he said, "Does the world really care about my hair?"

"Image is *everything*, Jagger. The goatee and moustache add sophistication, so I'll allow those. I'm touting you as the shiny, new Jagger Loving with the squeaky-clean reputation. What's my motto?"

He hated that she treated him like an errant child and rolled his eyes. "Help me help you."

The sedan pulled to the curb in front of an unremarkable Northwest DC office building that housed the American Hotel and Lodging Association. He ended the call, exited the vehicle, and walked inside.

If Jagger Loving had learned *anything* over the past year, it was not to screw his staff, his guests, or his clients. Something he used to do often and with vigor. The media might label him as God's gift to the hospitality industry, but he was the biggest fucker in the business and had been damned good at it. His playboy reputation tanked when someone mewled a little too loudly.

On his thirty-third birthday, he'd woken up buck naked and sandwiched between two equally nude female guests. After showing them out and comping their stay, he hoped they'd forget all about the wild night. But they wanted millions to keep quiet. He refused. They went public and a media frenzy followed. Unbeknownst to him, one of the women was married and the husband threatened to bash his head in. When the women threatened to publish *all* the photos and videos, the *real* issue became apparent.

His attorney had advised him to pay to make them go away. So he did. That had been the last straw. No more partying. No more late-night sexcapades. No more early-morning romps, either. Bad boy Jagger Loving had stopped, cold turkey.

Frustration burned a trail to his groin.

The hospitality industry meant everything to him. He'd built an empire from the ground up, and the sobering experience showed him how close he could come to losing it all.

When the daylong conference ended, the driver dropped him

at Sargent's in Georgetown for dinner. The top Zagat-rated restaurant had a six-month wait list. Leave it to his best friend, Maverick Hott, to wrangle them a table at the last-minute.

Jagger had barely stepped onto the sidewalk when Maverick bear-hugged him. "Jagger, baby!" One glance and his expression grew somber. "Christ, you look like you need to get laid, my friend."

Laughing, Jagger slapped his back. "You're insane, you know that? Let's go inside. My balls aren't used to these freezing temps."

His larger-than-life friend slung an arm over Jagger's shoulder and ushered him into the upscale eatery. Despite the wait, the host whisked them to a private dining room reserved for Washington's elite and friends of the owner.

Relaxing onto the cushioned chair, Jagger eyed the plush décor. "How'd you pull this off?"

"I made a call." Maverick dragged out a chair and sank down. "Jesus, I can't remember the last time I saw your ugly mug."

The host handed them menus as their server entered.

Jagger scanned the small plates. "Escargot and beef tartare. Mav, you good with that?"

"I'll eat whatever you order," Maverick said, before addressing the waiter. "Your top-shelf whiskey, neat, and a bottle of your finest sparkling water." With a tight smile, the attendant left.

"Hear about Colton's engagement?" Maverick asked, settling into the chair.

"I was so damn shocked, I was speechless," Jagger replied. "Brigit, right? Can she handle him?"

Crossing his legs, Maverick grinned. "He's a pussy-whipped goner." The two men laughed. "I have to admit, she's good for him. He's happy and that's a first."

"I'll meet her tomorrow. I'm stopping at Colton's on my way to the airport."

"Crockett's news is what threw me."

"What about him?" Jagger asked, dropping the cloth napkin on his lap.

"He got engaged."

Jagger laughed. "Sure he did. He's as engaged as I am. No, he's more like you, which means never."

"I'm serious. Alexandra Mitus came back into town. Another happy idiot."

"You aren't messin' with me?"

"No, brother, I swear."

Talking with Maverick had always been easy. They'd met freshman year at Harvard and had been close friends ever since. The server returned with their drinks, recited the chef's specials, and left.

"Welcome back, my friend." Maverick toasted Jagger before tossing back a mouthful of whiskey. "How are you doing? Don't bullshit me."

"I'm good." Jagger sipped his water. "Things have stabilized."

"I'm glad to hear that. You got my keys?"

After pulling the ring from his pocket, Jagger set it on the table. "Your cabin was perfect. I owe you one."

"Nah, it was the least I could do. You needed to get away." Maverick stashed the keys in his coat. "I go there to clear my head. After the stress of a mission, I need silence."

"Been in the Middle East lately?"

"Yeah, and I'm headed back there."

"I know you can't talk here. Be careful."

"Thank you, bro. Always am." Maverick tossed back another mouthful. "Looks like you're out of the media hot seat."

"For the most part. Now, I work all the time, especially before a hotel opens. You coming to visit?"

"Hell, yeah, but I can't make it for your grand opening. In two weeks, right?"

"No, next week. Valentine's Day."

"Good luck. You'll do great."

When a different server delivered their appetizers, Maverick grinned. "Hello, beautiful. Pull up a chair and join us."

A pinkish hue covered her cheeks. "Is there anything else you need, gentlemen?"

"Hell, yeah, how 'bout a blow—"

"*No*," Jagger interrupted. "Thank you."

Her eyes never strayed from Maverick, a smile tugging at the corners of her mouth. "Yes, sir," she replied, and left the room.

Jagger slid the raw meat dish closer. "You're crazy, you know that, right?"

Another grin split Maverick's face. "Certifiable, but I think she would have done it."

Chuckling, Jagger sliced off a piece of tartare. "Doesn't it get old?"

Holding the shell with the tongs, Maverick forked out an escargot and popped the delicacy into his mouth. He chewed, swallowed. "Yes and no. So many sexy chicks, but Colton and Crockett's engagements got me thinking." Maverick shrugged. "Then a cutie crosses my path and, well, I've gotta have her…"

The men laughed. "At least you're getting some," Jagger said.

"Hit a dry spell?"

"Like the goddamn Sahara."

"If you're not playing with the ladies, what *are* you doing?"

"Work, golf," Jagger said. "I'm frustrated as hell."

The pretty server returned with a finger's worth of whiskey. "Compliments of the house." She set the drink in front of Maverick and handed him a folded piece of paper. "Text me sometime."

He slipped the note into his inside breast suit pocket. "I'm keeping this close to my heart, darlin'."

After refilling Jagger's sparkling water, she shot Maverick a flirty smile and exited.

"You aren't going to call her," Jagger said.

"Probably not." After a pause, Maverick asked, "How long are you in DC?"

"Flying out late tomorrow."

"Let's see if we can do some damage between now and then." Maverick raised his glass.

Jagger toasted his friend. "I'll drink to that."

Over an hour later, they left the restaurant.

"I've got my Porsche," Maverick said, after handing the valet his ticket. "I'll drop you at the hotel."

"I'm hosting a party for VIP suppliers and clients in my suite," Jagger said. "Why don't you join me? I won't be hooking up with any of the ladies, but I'm sure you'll find someone warm to cozy up to for a few hours. Just do *not* screw her in my bed."

"I'm in," Maverick said.

Maverick pulled up in front of Hotel X and left the car with the valet. "What time does your party start?"

"Nine thirty," Jagger replied, walking into the boutique property.

Maverick checked his watch. "We've got plenty of time." He stopped at the concierge desk. "Hello, my good man. What's the word?"

The thin man smiled warmly. "Sir?"

"What's happening? You know, got any events worthy of a pop-in here in swanky-ville?"

"Ah, yes," said the concierge. "We have a masquerade charity event in the main ballroom."

"Are there women at this fundraiser?" Maverick asked.

Looking over his reading glasses, the hotel employee chuckled. "Yes, sir, I believe I saw several of them head in that direction. We're expecting over two hundred."

"What's the charity?" Maverick asked.

"*Walk a Mile in My Shoes*," said the employee. "It's a —"

"I know that charity," Jagger said. "They champion the homeless. Let's go check it out."

2

THE AUCTION

A s Taylor Hathaway stood in the small salon off the ballroom in the upscale Georgetown hotel, she wanted to smack her fellow volunteer across his drunken, masked face. An hour ago, he'd arrived sober. Now, he was totally inebriated and completely incapable of emceeing the event.

"I kin totally do this, Tayyy-lor-r-r." Spencer swayed and snickered. "No prob."

Taylor grabbed the microphone, made sure it was switched off, and pointed. "Sit in that chair. Do not move."

For the past several months, Taylor had poured every free moment into this fundraiser. As a volunteer for *Walk a Mile in My Shoes*, she wanted the evening to garner as much money as possible for the DC-based charity.

Melissa Rodriguez, *Walk a Mile's* executive director, lined up the auction participants before bee-lining over. "How's he doing?"

"He's shit-faced." Taylor bit back a scream. "There's no way he can stand up in front of an audience and manage to say anything coherent."

"Can he read the index cards?" Melissa asked.

The two women eyed Spencer. He sat on the floor, propped against the wall, laughing hysterically.

"Does that answer your question?" Taylor said. "Ohmygod, this is bad. What are we going to do?"

Melissa peeked into the ballroom. "The good news is that we're standing-room only. The bad is that we don't have a plan B." With her hands on her hips, she eyed Taylor. "I've got it. You're going to emcee."

Adrenaline spiked through her. "*What*? No way. I can't get up in front of those people." Taylor thrust the mic at Melissa. "You're cool, calm, *and* the executive director. You do it."

Refusing to take the microphone, Melissa crossed her arms. "I have to manage everything else. That includes making sure our bachelors and bachelorettes don't get drunk while they're waiting to go onstage."

Taylor's hands grew clammy while her heart hammered in her chest. "I…I can't. I'm sorry."

With a scowl, the director surveyed the other volunteers. "I don't trust anyone else like I trust you. We don't have a choice." She stepped close and put her arm around Taylor. "Sweetie, the guests will be focused on our bachelors and bachelorettes. And they've been tossing back a few." She shot Spencer a dirty look. "Hopefully, not that much, but maybe enough to be generous with their bids. We set a goal to raise twenty-five thousand dollars *in one night*. That money can help a *lot* of people. *You* can help a lot of people, Taylor."

Taylor didn't want to let anyone down, but Melissa was asking the impossible. "I cannot—as in, *no* way—stand in front of that crowd, let alone speak to them. I'm a nervous wreck just thinking about it." She shoved her shaking hand in Melissa's face.

"You look phenomenal." Melissa stepped back to examine Taylor. "All glammed up is definitely your thing. Your updo is stunning. Who's going to recognize you in that mask, anyway? Pretend you're someone else."

"Melissa, I can't do this."

"You're poised."

"No, I'm not."

"You're fierce, like a lioness."

"Hardly. I'm a mouse."

Melissa adjusted her own mask before grasping Taylor's arm. "This is your opportunity to do something really wonderful for a group of individuals who are counting on us. All you have to do is read what's on these cards. Please, Taylor, I'm begging you."

Peering through the door at the audience, Taylor murmured, "I'm going to pass out." She sucked in a shaky breath, unable to stop trembling.

"Taylor, look at me." Melissa squeezed her shoulders and stared into her eyes. "Life is all about making bold choices. Make this moment *bold*."

Before Taylor had a chance to dig her stilettos into the carpet, Melissa walked her into the ballroom and up on stage. Forcing herself to peek at the audience, Taylor grew rigid. Row after row of guests filled the ballroom. Most wore masquerade masks and everyone was dressed to impress. *Ohmygod, ohmygod. Breathe.*

Melissa grasped Taylor's hand, still cemented around the mic, raised it to her mouth, and flipped the switch. "Good evening, ladies and gentlemen." Melissa grinned at the waiting crowd. "I'm Melissa Rodriguez, executive director for *Walk a Mile in My Shoes,* and this is my gorgeous cohost—"

"*Raven,*" Taylor blurted into the mic. Her heart thundered so hard she couldn't hear anything else. "W-w-we're all here because we—" Her mind blanked.

"Yes, that's right, *Raven.* Homelessness affects more than just those in need of a jumpstart. Tonight, your generosity will make a positive difference by helping them get back on their feet. We have gorgeous bachelors and bachelorettes who are generously auctioning themselves for a date with you." Melissa grinned at the audience. "Bid a lot and bid *big*. Are you ready to get this party started?"

"Yes!" the group shouted, applauding enthusiastically.

"Then, let's do this." Melissa let go of Taylor's hand, and the mic clunked onto the stage.

Mortified, Taylor snatched it up. Melissa handed her the stack of index cards before hurrying offstage.

Gaping at the audience, she struggled for words. Two hundred guests packed the room. All eyes on her. *The cards. Use the cards.* She shifted her gaze to the short stack in her unsteady hand and willed herself to speak.

"First up is…" Her upper lip quivered. She took a few steps and her ankle wobbled in the stiletto. She stumbled, but kept herself from falling flat on her face. Several in the audience laughed. *This is beyond humiliating.* Then, Taylor thought of her Auntie Patty and how proud she'd be. If only she could push past her fear. *Do this for her. Do this for Patty.*

The cards shook in her quaking hand, but she forced herself to read the words printed on them. "Our first bachelor is sure to be a hit."

The cued music began while a handsome man in a dark suit emerged onstage and struck a model's pose.

"Trevor is all muscle and no fat," Taylor continued reading. "He's ready to talk about scuba diving or take you on a mountain hike. And if your muscles are sore at the end of the day, he's more than happy to rub the tension away—Oh my, who can resist that? —Bidding starts at five hundred dollars, but this fine man is worth much more than that."

Though she sounded stilted and she still hadn't smiled, her trembling had subsided a little. The focus of attention had shifted to Trevor, who strutted across the stage like he owned it.

A woman seated in the second row, wearing a feathered masquerade mask, raised her hand. "Five hundred."

Muscles running down Taylor's shoulders loosened. "Thank you. How about six hundred?"

Another hand shot up. "Six."

"Thank you. Do I hear seven-fifty?"

Trevor removed his suit jacket, draped it over his shoulder, and struck a different pose. Hoots and hollers filled the room.

Bidding for this bachelor stopped at one thousand. They'd never reach their goal at this rate, but the event had just started. Trevor left the stage as the first bachelorette strolled on. Taylor envied her confident smile and sexy catwalk.

I'm Raven. No one knows me. Taylor forced a smile before reading the card. "Delaney is a pediatrician by day, but if you play your date right, she'll play doctor with you at night. Let's start the bidding at eight hundred."

⸻

JAGGER DIDN'T WANT TO take his eyes off the pretty emcee, but he had to make sure someone could cover for him when his guests arrived. After receiving confirmation that his VP of global sales was waiting in Jagger's suite, he replied that he'd been detained.

Initially, he'd wanted to jump onstage and hold Raven's hand, put his arm around her—anything—to help calm her down. Current bidding on the first bachelorette had reached two thousand dollars. That seemed to bolster Raven's confidence. Her tight shoulders relaxed and her quivering voice subsided.

Though in heels, she appeared about average height. But there was nothing else average about her. Even from the back of the room, he liked what he saw. Dark bangs covered her forehead and an ornate masquerade mask framed her eyes. He appreciated her elegant neck and bare shoulders. Her black gown hugged her figure and he wanted a closer look. As an avid runner, he was a sucker for a lean, muscular woman, and the lovely Raven fit the bill to a T.

"She's lovely," he murmured under his breath.

"Throw out a bid," Maverick said as he leaned against the back wall.

"I'm talking about the emcee."

"Hmm, I figured you'd go for the one parading around on stage."

"No. There's something about Raven..." With a smile, Jagger shrugged.

"Be right back." After punching Jagger's shoulder, Maverick left the ballroom.

Several minutes later, Maverick returned. Jagger tossed his friend a nod, but his attention was diverted when Raven squealed. A round of chuckles floated through the audience. The current bachelor, wearing tuxedo pants and suspenders over his bare chest, had whisked her into his arms.

"Thank you, Sven," Raven said. "Why don't you show off those big muscles for the ladies, but put me down *first*."

Another wave of laughter filled the room.

As the bachelor flexed and posed like Mr. Universe, Raven read his stats from the card. When the bidding stopped at twenty-nine hundred, her smile lit up her face.

A wave of heat infused Jagger's chest. *She's adorable.*

The next bachelorette moseyed onto the stage.

"Ladies and gentlemen, Mattie is open to an evening with either gender. So, if a beautiful blonde with a passion for dogs is something you're interested in, I urge you to raise your hand and be generous with your bid."

"I like doggie style." Maverick's booming voice filled the ballroom. He stepped up behind the last row and threw up his arm. "Three thousand."

Raven's jubilant grin sent adrenaline shooting through Jagger. *Damn, she's hot.*

The intense bidding continued, until a masked woman won

with a bid of forty-five hundred. Maverick returned to his spot against the wall beside Jagger.

"Why didn't you bid to win?" Jagger whispered.

With a casual shrug, Maverick said, "Didn't want her that badly. Thought it would be fun to up the bidding, though."

Over the next thirty minutes, Jagger stayed focused on Raven. She'd calmed down enough to lend her personality to the auction. In addition to making the audience laugh, she kept the event moving along.

After the show, he wanted to introduce himself, but he had to get upstairs. According to a recent text from his VP, several guests were anxious to see him. Jagger could only make them wait so long before they'd leave, taking their valuable business with them.

"Congratulations to the winners and let's put our hands together for our amazing bachelors and bachelorettes," Raven said. "Ladies and gentlemen, thank you for your generosity. For everyone at *Walk a Mile*, we are so grateful. Homelessness is a problem that we can solve *together*. You're welcome to stay in the ballroom or continue your party at the hotel bar. Would the winners please rendezvous in the salon behind me? You can meet your date and exchange contact information."

"Wait!" Melissa hurried onstage and snatched the mic. "Someone was added with a starting bid of five thousand!"

"Great," Raven exclaimed. "Could that person join us on stage?"

"It's you." With an exuberant smile, Melissa addressed the audience. "Before we start the bidding, please help me thank Raven for emceeing. Didn't she do a fantastic job?"

While Melissa led the audience in applause, Jagger pushed off the wall.

"Gentlemen, this is your opportunity to spend time with one of the sweetest, smartest and most generous women I know," Melissa continued. "And she's beautiful, too. Take off your mask so our audience can see who they're bidding on."

"My mask?" Taylor squeaked out.

Melissa nodded.

As Taylor removed her mask, her confidence fizzled. She hadn't gone on a date in a long time, and she had no interest in going on one with a stranger.

"Do I hear a bid of fifty-one hundred?" Melissa began.

"Happy birthday, Jagger." Maverick nudged him. "Place your bid or you'll lose her."

"Fifty-one," yelled a masked man seated near the front.

"Six thousand," called another.

"Jesus, do I have to bid for you?" Maverick thrust Jagger forward.

Now standing behind the last row, Jagger raised his hand. "Sixty-five."

"Seven," hollered the first man.

"Seventy-eight," Jagger replied.

"Eight," said the first man.

"Nine," Jagger shouted.

"Ten," the other bidder yelled.

Jagger had had enough. Time to shut down this bidding war. "Twenty."

The room went silent. Everyone spun in their seats. Jagger's smile was more reactionary than sincere. He'd stunned himself. It's not like he didn't have the money, it was more about the fact that he wasn't about to let Raven get away.

"Great Zeus!" Melissa exclaimed.

Raven's mouth dropped open.

"Going once," Melissa said. "Going twice." She paused. "Going thrice to the handsome gentleman standing in the back."

"Ohmygod," Raven murmured, the mic catching her shock.

"That was one hell of a finale, wouldn't you agree?" Melissa asked, and the audience broke into laughter and applause.

When the room quieted down, Melissa continued. "On behalf of *Walk a Mile in My Shoes*, we are extremely thankful. One hundred percent of tonight's proceeds are earmarked for the homeless. Please check our website to track where your donation goes and for those who would like to pledge a donation, we welcome any and all contributions. No amount is too small. Again, for those who've won, please join us in the salon. Thank you, safe travels, and good night." And with that, Melissa switched off the mic.

Maverick slapped Jagger on the back. "I'm happy to split this with you. I didn't think that guy would push you like that."

"It's not about the money," Jagger said. "What in the hell possessed you to do that?"

"After listening to you at dinner, I wanted to get you something *special* for your birthday. Happy birthday, brother. Let's go meet Raven."

3

THE INVITATION

A s soon as Taylor entered the salon, she grabbed her clutch and flew down the hallway to the restroom, her heart fluttering like a hummingbird. *Some man paid twenty thousand dollars for a date with me.* Taylor entered the stall, lifted her gown, and plunked her ass on the toilet.

When she emerged, several guests were freshening their makeup.

"You did a phenomenal job," said one woman. "That pretend tripping was funny! I wish I had your comedic flair."

She's just being polite. While washing her hands, Taylor smiled. "Thanks for saying that and thank you for coming. Did you win a bachelor?"

"No, but I'm headed back into the salon to donate a little something. I don't have that kind of money to bid."

"You're married," interrupted her friend. "You're not supposed to bid."

Everyone in the bathroom laughed, including Taylor, and her racing pulse slowed.

"Seriously," said the first woman. "I envy you. Did you see the guy who won you?"

After drying her hands, Taylor fluffed her bangs. "Not really. He was all the way in the back."

"Oh, honey, he's gorgeous," said the second woman. "That man is total eye candy." Talking amongst themselves, the women paraded out.

Handsome? Hmm, maybe he did it on a dare. Taylor glossed her lips before leaving. As she approached the salon, her chest tightened. Good-looking men turned her into a bundle of jumbled nerves. But this man had bid on *Raven.* As far as he was concerned, timid Taylor didn't exist. Melissa's mantra echoed in her head. *Life is all about making bold choices.*

Emboldened by her brave alter ego, she threw back her shoulders. For the sake of the charity, she could fake it for the next ten minutes while she thanked the winner and gave him her phone number. But once he got a close look at her, he'd bail. *He's probably trashed, like Spencer.*

Seconds after she entered the salon, Melissa waved her over to the collection table.

"There you are!" Melissa beamed. "Congratulations, you killed it. Thank you so, so much. The event was a huge success because of you!"

"Team effort," corrected Taylor.

"Excuse me," said a deep voice behind her.

She turned and her heart leapt into her throat. A gorgeous man, with flashing hazel eyes and full lips, smiled. Dark hair hung over one eyebrow, giving him a devil-may-care appearance. Her brain shorted.

"You did a great job tonight, Raven." His smooth-as-silk timbre rumbled through her, and a whoosh of heat burned a trail down to her toes.

Right, I'm Raven. "Thank you," she murmured.

His closely cropped goatee and moustache drew her attention back to his sexy mouth. *A man like that is used to supermodels and corporate execs.* Those types of women exuded confidence and grace. She possessed neither.

She scooted around the table to take his payment. "Did you want to pledge a donation?"

"I won a bachelorette."

"Congratulations. Who did you win?"

His beautiful smile sent her pulse soaring. "I won you."

She stilled. This had to be a joke. *No way did this man bid twenty thousand on me.*

"Thanks to me," boasted the grinning man next to him.

Her heart dropped as she forced a smile at the linebacker-sized friend. Her suspicions had been spot-on. *They'd gotten into that bidding war as a joke.* Striking men like these didn't pay attention to ordinary girls like her.

But what difference did that make? He'd paid a ton of money for an evening with Raven. And so what if she was the brunt of some joke? She'd shoulder it for the sake of helping a lot of people get back on their feet.

With a relaxed smile, the winner extended his hand. "Jagger Loving."

When she slipped hers into his large one, sparks zipped through her. As they stared into each other's eyes, she felt like she'd found the missing puzzle piece.

"Hellooooo, people," said the friend. "I'm here, too, you know."

"My friend, Maverick Hott," Jagger said as his phone rang. "Excuse me." He answered. "What's the word?" He listened. "Be there in five."

She stiffened. *Of course he's gotta bolt. He has no interest in me.* "I don't want to keep you. Did you make arrangements to complete your donation?"

"Already paid it," he replied. "I donate annually to *Walk a Mile,* so Melissa found me in the database."

"That's great. Well, thank you again."

Jagger reached across the table and wrapped a strong hand

around her arm. His possessive hold sent a rush of heat over her face. She wished she didn't blush so easily.

"I'm hosting a business event in my suite. I'm running late, but wanted to introduce myself. Join us. You're welcome to bring Melissa. I need a way to contact you, but if I don't leave now, my guests are going to walk and take their business with them."

Taylor hesitated. She wasn't comfortable heading upstairs, no matter how handsome he was, or how much money he'd donated.

Melissa hurried over. "Thank you again, Jagger," she said, batting her eyelashes. Melissa, who never looked twice at another man, grinned. "And thank you for the invitation. As soon as I'm finished here, my husband, Don, and I will join you in your suite. That was so nice of you to include us."

"Glad you can make it." Jagger smiled at Taylor and a zing of attraction skittered through her. "Bring Raven with you."

"Have you two exchanged contact info?" Melissa asked.

"No, which is why you need to promise me that she'll be there. Presidential suite, top floor."

Nodding like a love-struck fool, Melissa said, "You have my word."

As soon as the men left, Melissa placed her hand over her heart. "Gorgeous doesn't even begin to describe those two."

Taylor glared at her. "You did not just swoon. What is wrong with you?"

She grinned at Taylor. "Nothing, now."

"I've never seen you act like this."

"That man paid twenty thousand dollars for a date with you. What's wrong with *you*?"

"He could be a serial killer for all we know."

Melissa waved her off. "Google him. Meet him for dinner. Bring a friend. Tell your mother. You live with twenty people in a damned commune. Tell them."

Laughing, Taylor said, "I don't live in a commune."

"Let's finish up here, grab Don, and get upstairs. I'm starving.

My money says Mr. Loving has some scrumptious treats awaiting us. And I'm not even talking about the food!"

Twenty minutes later, Taylor rode the elevator with Melissa and her husband. "So, the man who won you thinks your name is Raven," said Don. "And since you're not telling him the truth, I can't call you Taylor."

"Right," she replied. "And if he or his friend asks about me, don't tell them anything. Deflect all questions. Promise?"

With a sheepish grin, Don adjusted his bifocals. "He paid twenty *thousand* dollars. Trust me, he's interested in you."

"It's a joke or a dare." Taylor glared at them. "I'm counting on you two."

"No worries," Melissa said.

The elevator opened and they piled out. "Don and I are staying long enough to have a quick bite. We splurged on a night here." She threaded her fingers through her husband's hand as they headed toward the suite.

The door was open, so they moseyed inside. Taylor hadn't taken three steps when Maverick bustled over.

"Hey! You made it. Maverick Hott." He shook Don's hand. "Pretty sweet digs. Let me show you the spread." He escorted them through the art deco living room and into the equally stylish dining area. "There's beer, wine, soda, sparkling water. What can I get everyone?"

Taylor wanted to suck down a ginger ale in the hopes of calming her stomach, but that would be a dead giveaway she was a wreck. "Sparkling water. No, I'll have a glass of red wine, please."

Tonight, Raven was in charge and she drank alcohol. Maverick poured from a bottle of Cabernet Sauvignon that Taylor suspected cost a few hundred dollars. *Who is this Jagger Loving?*

She glanced around the spacious suite filled with people and her heart skipped a beat when she spied him. Though he stood in a small group, he turned in her direction, as if he knew exactly where she was. The second they connected, her pulse pounded a frenetic rhythm. He broke eye contact long enough to place his hand on the arm of the man to his right, say something that left everyone chuckling, and head in her direction.

A raw hunger lurked in his eyes. With his every step, her insides burned with desire. Even though she squirmed from his intense energy, she couldn't turn away. *I'm Raven. Cool, sophisticated Raven.* Knowing she could play the part of someone else calmed her down. She turned and faced him.

"I'm glad you could make it." Jagger placed his hand on her arm. That simple touch excited her in a myriad of ways. "You look beautiful."

He sounded so sincere; she wanted to believe him. "Thank you and thanks for inviting us." She gestured to her friends, but Melissa and Don were chatting with Maverick while filling their plates at the buffet table. She and Jagger stood alone. A tremble skirted through her.

Jagger tossed a nod toward the buffet. "I think your friends are hungry." Instead of following his gaze, she studied his profile. From every angle, he was gorgeous. High cheekbones and a strong jawline accentuated his chiseled face. As soon as she honed in on his sexy mouth, she pursed hers, but the whisper-soft moan still managed to escape.

Not wanting to get caught gawking, she peered into her glass. This man was so out of her league. Beyond his striking looks, he carried himself with a confidence she only dreamed about.

"You okay?" He ran a comforting hand from her shoulder blades to the small of her back, and kept it there.

Meeting his fiery gaze, she nodded. But she was crumbling from his intensity.

"I see you have something to drink. How about some food?" The heat from his fingers seeped through the lace gown. She could have stood like that forever.

"That's a good idea," she said, finding her voice. "It's been a long day."

With a plate in hand, Jagger escorted her through the buffet, ensuring she received a sampling of several delicious-looking foods. Then, he seated her at the dining room table, retrieved her utensils, a bottle of sparkling water and two glasses, and joined her. Despite feeling self-conscious, she loved how he waited on her.

"Are you eating?" she asked as he eased onto the chair, catty-corner from hers.

"Maverick and I had a huge meal at Sargent's." He poured their waters and lifted his glass. "Cheers. Congratulations on a successful event. Melissa said you really came through for her."

"Thank you," she murmured, unable to look away. She could hardly breathe, but her insides were humming. Taylor became tongue tied around handsome, sophisticated men like Jagger, but she had to say something. "Did you arrive late to the fundraiser?" *That was brilliant.*

"We got there when you took the stage."

She wanted to ask, *why me?* Instead, she bit off the end of a lobster toast with avocado, and the tiny cracker crumbled onto the plate. *C'mon get it together.* She nibbled a carrot tart with ricotta and almond filling. This gorgeous, elegant man deserved his money's worth, starting right now. Swallowing down a mountain of insecurities, she pinned on a smile.

"What do you do?" she asked.

"I'm in the hospitality industry. How about you? Do you work full-time for *Walk a Mile?*"

"No, I'm..." *What does Raven do?* Her mind raced with possibilities. "I'm a vet...primarily dogs," she blurted. "Cats, fish, too." *Ohgod, I'm losing it.* She forced a laugh. "No, no fish."

He chuckled, but he hadn't stopped staring at her. Assuming she had food on her face, she wiped the corners of her mouth with the cloth napkin.

"Well, Doctor, I'm impressed you'd volunteer with what must be a full schedule."

Tell him the truth, apologize, give him your phone number, and leave. He'll never call.

"We're heading out," someone said.

Taylor continued staring into Jagger's eyes. "I…so…um, I'm not really a…the reason I intro—"

"*Raven.* We're leaving."

Taylor whipped her head toward Melissa. "Congratulations on a successful evening," she said, and popped out of her seat.

"I'll circulate a press release in the AM." Melissa smiled at Jagger. "Would you mind if I highlight your generous contribution?"

He rose. "If publicizing my donation would benefit the organization, go ahead."

Don shook Jagger's hand. "Thank you for including us." He nodded at Taylor. "Great job tonight, *Raven.*"

As Taylor hugged Don goodbye, her thoughts were on the major lie she'd just told. She didn't know the first thing about being a veterinarian and wished she'd blurted out something closer to her actual career. Or simply told him the truth.

Melissa hugged her. "I Googled him for you," she whispered. "He's yummy. Have fun." She shot Jagger one more smile before Don ushered her toward the door.

Taylor felt lightheaded and grabbed the table's edge for support. She was in over her head.

"Okay, time to eat." Jagger held the chair for her and she eased back down.

To her surprise, he stabbed the delicate greens and held out the fork. She took the utensil from him and ate. As she peered into his eyes, Melissa's voice echoed in her head like a mantra. *Life is all about making bold choices. Make this moment bold.* She made a decision. For one night, she'd be someone she wasn't—confident, brave, brash. Raven had gotten her through the event. Raven could take her the rest of the way, too.

"How are you familiar with our charity?" she asked.

"I've donated to *Walk a Mile* for years." Jagger broke eye contact for a few seconds. "When I was a child, my family experienced homelessness, so I know, firsthand, it's a struggle to turn things around." Sadness banked in his eyes before he shrugged a shoulder. "Not something I usually discuss."

Her heart stopped. She'd not expected that answer from a man who oozed wealth and charm. More than that, she'd not anticipated that level of disclosure. Guilt floated over her like an angry storm cloud. He didn't even know her real name and he thought she was a vet. "I'm sorry," she murmured.

"It was a long time ago." That smooth-as-silk voice rumbled through her. "Now I'm in a position to help others. Plus, I won the auction's most beautiful woman, so I'd say I'm the envy of the fundraiser." His sexy smile shot her pulse into the stratosphere.

No man had ever said anything that compelling, that powerful, about her.

Her breath caught in her throat. "Thank you," she murmured. "I'm not worthy." She wished she hadn't said that.

"Why would you say that?" He picked up the lone marinated olive and offered her the tiny black fruit. "I'm a firm believer in the clean plate club." This time, she opened her mouth. When he slipped it inside, his thumb caressed her bottom lip. Her skin tingled, and his low, husky moan sent a jolt straight to her core.

"What about you?" he asked. "Is homelessness personal for you, too?"

Taylor hesitated. *What is Raven's story?* Should she offer a nugget of truth? *Be honest.*

"My Auntie Patty lived with us off and on throughout my childhood. She was awesome and I adored her. She suffered from mental illness, but I never knew. When I was in college, she died homeless. I always thought that if I'd known, I could have helped her somehow." She'd never shared that with anyone and the loss filled her with a sudden jolt of grief. At least she'd told Jagger something truthful about herself.

"I'm sorry," he said.

"Jagger, pardon the interruption." A stocky man extended his hand. "This was great."

"Excuse me," Jagger said to Taylor before pushing out of his chair and shaking the man's hand. "My pleasure. Glad you could make it."

The man smiled. "Must feel great to be back."

Jagger nodded. "Sensational, actually."

Back from where?

Several more guests ambled over to express their thanks before heading out. It was after eleven. She hadn't had time to process the whirlwind evening, much less accept that she was sitting with a man who'd paid twenty thousand dollars for *her*.

As Jagger said goodbye to the last client, Taylor rose. It might have been the passion in his eyes, or the way that lock of hair shadowed his brow, or how he offered her a charming smile. But she didn't want to leave.

"You're not heading out, too, are you?" Before she had a chance to respond, he stepped close. "Stay."

That word tumbled through her. No man had ever spoken to her in such a commanding tone. Unable to tear herself away, she stared into his bright eyes.

"Brother, we're outta here." Maverick hijacked their moment.

Taylor acknowledged the woman superglued to his arm. As the two friends said their goodbyes, her mind wandered.

Though she'd never had a one-night stand, she wouldn't let this opportunity pass her by. Jagger was different from the men she'd dated. He oozed worldly sophistication and an abundance of confidence. He was fascinating and attentive, and flat-out gorgeous. Plus, she got the impression he wasn't even from around here, so she didn't have to worry about seeing him again. *What would Raven do?*

Raven would take full advantage of this situation. Raven, the veterinarian, didn't even have a last name and she'd keep it that way. A smile tugged at the corners of her mouth. *One evening of bold choices and no regrets.*

But someone should know, so she pulled her phone from her clutch and texted Melissa. "I'm staying in Jagger's suite. I'll text you in the morning so you know I'm alive."

Tiny dots appeared. "Have fun! That's an order!"

No regrets. She slipped her phone back into her purse.

The two men clasped hands. "Great to see you," Jagger said to Maverick before addressing the woman still clutching his friend's arm. "Let me know when you're headed west and I'll roll out the red carpet."

The woman smiled. "Everything about your resorts are red carpet, but I appreciate the invitation."

Resorts? Taylor glanced at him.

"Congrats on tonight, Raven." Maverick winked at Jagger before heading out, the fawning blonde in tow.

Alone with Jagger. The air turned electric. When she redirected her attention, he pierced her with a heated gaze. Energy whizzed through her.

All of him taking in all of her solidified her decision. She couldn't wait to get him naked and run her hands over every sexy inch of him. Knowing her identity was safe behind a fictitious character—one with no past, no present, and no future—bolstered her confidence. Raven had one night and Taylor was going to take full advantage of it...and of him. Her insides vibrated with an ache that had her pressing her thighs together.

Knock. Knock.

"Unbelievable," he said. Rather than leaving Taylor in the dining room, Jagger held her hand. "Something tells me you're a flight risk." She laughed. "I'd handcuff you to me if I had a pair."

Ohmygod. I would love that.

He walked with purpose toward the door, Taylor floating alongside. Did her feet even touch the floor? Her hand fit snugly in his. Did he realize that he was stroking her skin with his thumb? Was that also part of the Jagger Loving charm? Did all the ladies receive this smooth treatment? If he was anything like his friend, he was a major player. But Raven didn't care about any of that. Raven only cared about Raven and everything she'd never experienced. One night of wild passion with a sexy stranger.

Jagger opened the door.

Room service. The attendants followed them into the suite.

"Please leave any food that doesn't need refrigeration. Take the alcohol. We'll keep the sparkling water."

Was he one of those people who spoke in the plural or had he purposefully included the "we" for her benefit? She'd become hypersensitive to his every move, his every word. And every time he looked in her direction, which he was doing again, she couldn't help but stare back. Who wouldn't? He was flawless, gorgeous, and sublimely sexy. And about to get fucked. Big time.

Only one question remained. Could Taylor play by Raven's carefree rules?

4

THE DECISION

J AGGER'S ATTRACTION TO RAVEN was off the charts. When she'd strolled into his suite, he knew he had to have her. She was strikingly gorgeous. Her ocean blue eyes hypnotized him. Her beautiful smile sent him rocketing to the moon. One minute she oozed confidence, the next, she seemed completely unsure, to the point of being downright timid.

And that's when he wanted to comfort her. Her sweet nature drew him in and kept him rooted by her side.

Before she'd arrived, he'd made a point to speak with every guest. Sure, he rushed things a bit, but he'd kicked up the charm, offered a warm smile, and a firm handshake. Most clients had been there to check a box or ensure themselves an invitation to Loving Malibu. And he hadn't disappointed. Everyone had received an engraved invitation for a complimentary two-night stay for two. Jagger may have arrived late to his own party, but his business associates had left happy.

The second he'd seen Raven, he couldn't get to her fast enough. An hour later, they were almost alone. Ten minutes until the hotel staff cleared out.

With his fingers still laced with hers, Jagger returned to the living room. Though he'd continued stroking her skin with his thumb, she'd turned rigid in his grasp. He had to play this right. She hadn't even given him her phone number. But he was a realist. He had just dropped anchor in California and she lived in the DC area. Even with all the technology at their disposal, nothing replaced human contact. He didn't want a long-distance relationship. In the long run, it wouldn't work, especially from the get-go. But he had tonight and he was damn well going to make the most of it.

Their chemistry was undeniable. He hated looking anywhere but at her. She smelled feminine and flowery. She was sexy as hell, not just physically, but emotionally, too. Part timid, part bold was his hot button. He gestured for her to sit on the sofa.

She remained standing. "So, you're from out of town." Disappointment tinged her voice.

"Yes. I had an association meeting in DC."

"Where do you live?" When she pulled her hand from his, a chill ran through him.

"I recently moved to California." He didn't touch her again, on purpose.

Arching a brow, she broke eye contact. A few seconds later, she stepped close enough for him to appreciate the faint smell of her arousal.

"How can you claim your prize if you don't live around here?" Her voice had dropped. She stopped fidgeting. A sense of calm and determination streamed from her eyes.

"And what, exactly, is my prize, Raven?"

Her gaze floated over his face, pausing on his mouth. Her breathing had shifted and her lips parted.

"I am."

More than anything, he wanted to haul her into his arms and kiss her, then drive himself inside her until they both surrendered to the ecstasy. And then, he wanted to do it again. Stopping only when the morning light streamed through the hotel windows.

"Excuse me, Mr. Loving," said the head attendant. "We're done, sir. Have a good evening." The staff left, quietly closing the suite door behind them.

But Jagger hadn't paid for a fuck and he wanted to make that perfectly clear. If need be, he'd walk. Wouldn't be the first time.

"Raven, that's not why I invited you here—"

Her mouth was on his, her arms wrapping his back, stroking him with a raw, ravenous need that sent energy pounding his groin. Their breathing quickened. The kiss was greedy, reckless, and rough.

Groaning into her, he opened his mouth and she pressed her tongue to his. The grittiness of her throaty sounds turned the heat level way up. His pulse quickened, his cock throbbed against his boxers.

He threaded one hand around the back of her neck and anchored the other on her ass. This time, her whimper sent more blood to his aching erection while her fingers dug into his hair. Every urge commanded he yank up her gown and drive himself inside her. The intensity of their embrace demanded it. But for reasons he couldn't process in the heat of the moment, he didn't want to nail her. Not yet, anyway.

Breaking the kiss, he gasped for air. "Raven—" he growled. He needed to slow this down.

Her lips were red, ripe. Her bright eyes full of want. Her chest expanded with every labored breath. This woman would be his undoing and he couldn't become undone fast enough.

She came at him again, but this time the kiss was soft, tender. Her warm mouth melded to his and a tiny smile floated on her lips. He felt it and he saw it. Neither closed their eyes. He smiled back. Goddammit, he was always, always in control, especially in the bedroom, but this sweet, sexy woman had him hanging—dangling—on her every move.

"I have a proposition," she whispered. "One night. No

expectations. No strings. We share a fantasy. If the other agrees, we do it."

He drew her close. Kissed her. "Tell me. What do you need?"

She seemed to draw strength from that question. "You, in my mouth," she said with an urgency he hadn't expected. "And I want you on a beach."

That image turned his already hard cock to granite. "Come visit me in California. Lots of beautiful beaches to choose from."

Her playful expression fell. "Nothing past tonight, so we'll have to improvise." She stroked the cotton covering his erection. "Tell me your dirty dreams."

"Eating you until you beg for a release tops my list." He brushed his lips to hers. "Mirror sex. I want to watch us."

Her expression faltered. Maybe he'd said too much. "I'm not on the pill. I'll assume you have condoms."

He loved an honest, direct woman. Sadly, he'd encountered so few. He could let a little white lie here and there slip through the cracks, but over the years, he'd met women who'd fed him one hell of a story. But Raven put it all out there.

"I have a condom."

Her eyebrows shot up. "Just one?"

He drew her into his arms. "How many do you need?"

The uneasiness floated away with her smile. "Two. We each get one fantasy."

He loved how she was up for anything. With his arm around her lean waist, they entered the bathroom. He rifled through his Dopp kit, pulled out a three-pack, and shot her a playful grin. "You are too dressed for what I have in mind. Time to get you naked, Raven."

They returned to the bedroom and he turned off all of the lights, save for one shining above the fireplace. A quick tap on the remote, and the gas flames bathed the room in a warm, fiery glow.

"Thank you for leaving a light on."

The quiet appreciation in her voice surprised him. "I want to watch you unravel around me when I take you over the edge." Her raspy groan sent need pounding through him.

With their fingers still interlocked, he turned to face her. He paused, appreciating her elegance, her delicate neck, her soft curves. Her eyes had turned dark and her hungry mouth had parted.

Slowly, he embraced her, stroked her soft cheek with the back of his finger. "Being with you now has nothing to do with winning you at the auction. What I mean...I didn't win you to sleep with you." *Jesus, get it together.*

She leaned up to kiss him. "Thank you for saying that, but I want to be here, with you. I want to have sex with you." Again, she offered a shy smile. "Intimate relations sounds better. Let's call it that. I have no expectations beyond tonight. We're both adults, and from what I can tell, we're both sober."

"Yes, I'm quite sober."

"We don't even live on the same side of the country, so let's make the most of our time together. No strings. No regrets."

His chest tightened. Strangely, he didn't like the sound of that. But, as he leaned close, deep blue eyes as vast as the ocean peered up at him. His mouth found hers and he tightened his hold. This felt different. She felt different. The wild intensity with which she kneaded his shoulders was in stark contrast to the delicate way her tongue tangled with his. Raven didn't just ignite his desire, she made the flame burn stronger.

When the kiss came to a natural end, she turned around. "There's a hook at the top," she whispered.

He peeled off the dress and eyed her creamy skin. Beneath the silky black cloth, she wore a strapless pink bra with matching thong panties. With her back to him and her hair swept off her neck, he had a front-row seat to her beautiful backside. Long, lean, and breathtaking.

He kissed her shoulder, his lips lingering on her warm skin. His insides were on fire, but he could wait. Jagger loved pleasuring a woman until she shattered beneath him. Her tremble snapped him out of his fantasy and he nibbled her soft shoulder before she turned toward him.

"I don't have big boobs," she murmured.

"Neither do I," he replied, admiring her breasts.

Her giggle landed square in his heart. He kissed her again before brushing kisses from her jawline, down her neck, and across her chest. When he pressed his lips to the swell of her breast, he inhaled everything Raven. She smelled delicious. "Your breasts are beautiful." He removed her bra and tossed it aside. Her already swollen nipples plumped when he teased them with his thumbs. "They're not just beautiful, they're perfect." And he meant it.

He'd been with busty women. Some natural; others not. And he'd been with small-breasted women, too. Breasts had never been the deciding factor. The woman was. And this one was doing it for him in the best of ways. He left her panties on because he wanted them soaked when he was done teasing her. Adrenaline rocketed through him and his cock strained against his boxers.

He toed off his loafers before she helped him remove his suit jacket. With determination in her eyes, she loosened his tie enough to pull it over his head. She worked quickly, removing his shirt and tugging off his undershirt. Pants were removed in record time, and so were his boxers. She ran gentle fingers over his chest before a gentle nudge sent him backwards. As soon as he sat on the king bed, she knelt at his feet and removed his socks. Then, she peered up at him. The wild gleam in her eyes, coupled with the delicate way she stroked him, turned him to granite. Again, she'd taken control, and all he could do was absorb hit after hit of pleasure surging through him.

"I haven't tasted a man in a long time." She licked her lips. Her breathing roared in his ears. "I'm clean. How 'bout you?"

Her directness surprised him. Before he could check himself, he said, "I'm clean and I haven't been with anyone in a while, either." Talking about his sex life with his lovers never happened. For some reason, Raven's honesty prompted him to keep it real.

With one hand around the base of his shaft, she devoured him with her mouth, and sucked with an unexpected frenzy. He gritted his teeth as wave after wave of euphoria streaked through him. Groaning, he murmured, "Fuck, Raven, you feel good."

On a throaty moan, she slowed her wild assault. Her tender strokes and gentle licks teased him, and he leaned back on his elbows to watch. She had this sexy way of working him in, rolling her tongue around his head, and pulling him back out.

"Delicious." Her raspy voice sounded nothing like the terrified woman who'd stepped onstage. With a ravenous look in her eyes, she straddled him.

"I want you inside me when you come," she said, peering down at him.

Feeling intoxicated, he gazed up at her. Her beauty and free spirit sent needy shock waves pulsing through him. "You don't hold back, do you?"

"Not tonight." She shot him a sultry grin. "Where are the condoms?"

And that's when Jagger's brain kicked into overdrive. In one easy move, he flipped them, pinning her beneath him. His mouth found hers. He kissed her hard, mercilessly. His tongue stroked hers while he slipped a hand between her legs.

"Not yet," he said. "You aren't ready."

"How do you know?"

He caressed her pussy over her underwear. "Because your panties aren't drenched."

"Ohmygod," she murmured.

"I can't wait to taste the sweetest, most intimate part of you."

Her low, deep groan streaked desire through him.

With one hand claiming her breast, he kissed her until she writhed beneath him, then he suckled her swollen nipples until her moans turned into growls. He nibbled his way across her toned midriff until her ass lifted from the mattress. When he stroked the insides of her thighs, she finally gave him what he needed.

"Please, Jagger," she panted. "I can't hold on much longer. I need you inside me."

He felt the same way, but she hadn't climaxed yet. "Ladies first."

Off came her soaked panties. "This," he said, holding up the undergarment, "is you having fun."

With hooded eyelids, she reached for the three-pack. "Patience," he said, taking it from her. I'm hungry."

Her muffled cry tore through him and he fought the desire to plunge inside her. He hadn't wanted anyone this badly in…hell, he couldn't recall a time when he'd ever felt this kind of intoxicating pull from a woman. Whatever Raven possessed, he couldn't get enough of it.

He licked his lips, shouldered her legs apart, and pinned her with a hard stare. "I'm going to torture you until you beg for a release. And *then*, I'm going to fuck you."

With his mouth buried between her legs, he licked and sucked. He pulled back the hood of her clit and teased her delicate head. And he breathed sweet, sweet pussy. From a gentle flick of his tongue to slipping his fingers inside, he pleasured her until she fisted the sheet and gritted her teeth, writhing and groaning. Then, he slowed, and began the build again. When her body shook and her cries turned savage, she rasped out, "Jagger, I'm… I'm…ohhhhmyyyygod."

And she convulsed violently against his mouth. The intensity with which she responded to him only made him want her that much more.

She stilled, her taut body slowly relaxing. On a deep, soulful breath, her eyes fluttered open. He liked her sated, but he wasn't nearly done with her.

He pecked the soft curve of each hip before leaving a trail of kisses on her stomach, each breast, her chest, and, finally, her mouth.

"I need you inside me," she murmured.

He was done waiting. He turned up the lights over the fireplace, rolled on a condom, and returned to bed to find her on all fours. Energy streaked through his throbbing cock. While he stroked her curvy ass with one hand, he teased her soaked pussy with the other. Her raw, hungry sounds made him ache. "I want to see your expression when I enter you."

She moved so he could see her better in the mirrored wall. Their jagged breathing cut through the air as the swell of anticipation built to a frenzying state.

"*Please,*" she begged.

With cock in hand, he tunneled inside her soft flesh, their cries of pleasure piercing the silence. Her body bowed to his, but the thing that aroused him the most was that her eyes never left his. When he was nestled inside her, she started moving on him. It was then that she struggled to keep her eyes open.

"You feel so good," she rasped. "So good."

As he glided inside her, he stroked her back, her curvy ass. On another deep groan, she lowered her head.

He reached around and pinched her nipple. Shuddering in a ragged breath, she ground against him. "Faster. Harder."

As he thrust, the ecstasy overtook him. When she eyed him in the mirror, raw, untamed sexuality stared back. "You are so fucking hot." He gritted his teeth to keep from climaxing.

"I'm going to come," she said between gasps. "Come with me, Jagger."

He grabbed her hips and surrendered to the orgasm.

"Oh, god, yes," she choked out as she shattered around him.

Several glorious seconds passed before he pulled out. Didn't want to leave her heat, but he needed to kiss her more. Rising to her knees, she faced him, and wrapped her arms around his neck. He couldn't hold her tightly enough or kiss her long enough.

Maybe there was something in the DC water. Whatever it was, it was crazy. He wanted her again, but he needed time to recover.

When the embrace ended, he excused himself into the bathroom. He returned to find her snuggled beneath the linens. Joining her, he kissed her breathless.

"Your tattoo is beautiful," she said. "Can I see it?"

He flipped onto his stomach and she propped herself on her elbow. After studying it, she traced the outline from one shoulder blade to the other. Her tender touch both soothed and excited him.

"A phoenix?"

"Yes," he replied, rolling toward her.

"There must be a story behind that."

Leaning up, he kissed her. "I made some terrible choices. After turning my life around, I marked my new start with ink."

"Rising from the ashes," she murmured. "That's sexy. I don't have any tattoos." With a smirk, she added, "But I do have this fantasy." Her voice dropped to a whisper. "Lots of people have done it, but I haven't. Since my life is here, and I'm not traveling west anytime soon, I'd like to improvise, if you're up for a story."

"I'm up for anything you want to do." He tucked errant strands of hair behind her ear.

While she paused, he studied her face. Her delicate features—small nose, slender lips, and soulful eyes—were framed in her now mussed lion's mane.

"You're so beautiful." The words had spilled before he could censor them. One-night stands were all about the feels, but there was something special about this connection that tugged at his heart.

"You don't have to say that." She kissed him. "Imagine we're on a secluded beach," she began. "We're basking in the warm weather, our bodies moist with perspiration. The saltwater air is refreshing and you close your eyes. I roll on my stomach."

"What are you wearing?" he asked.

"A black bikini," she answers. "And I ask you to untie the straps so I don't have tan lines on my back."

Stroking her back, Jagger kissed her.

"You don't want me to burn, so you offer to rub sunscreen on me, but I roll onto my back, leaving the top on the blanket, and lean up on my elbows."

His cock twitched. "Aren't you a naughty girl?"

"Very," she replied, a wild gleam in her eyes.

They were lying sideways, facing each other, and she caressed his arm. He stroked her back, anchoring his hand to her curvy ass.

"While you suck my nipple, I whisper that I want you on the beach."

He groaned, his growing erection pressing against her. "Someone might see us," he said.

"That's a risk I'm willing to take. I need you, *Jagger*." Her husky moan sent a jolt of adrenaline through him. But it was *how* she murmured his name that turned him rock hard.

Breaking away, she felt around for a condom. "You remove your trunks while I wiggle out of my bikini bottoms." Her expression changed and she gave him a little smile. "No condom needed in my fantasy."

He smiled back and brushed a kiss over her lips. She ripped open the packet and he rolled it on. "I mount you and take you inside me."

Arousal thundered through him as she straddled him. The searing look in her eyes was eclipsed with a shyness he'd not expected.

"Fuck me on the beach," he commanded. She lifted up and took him inside her, working him into her most sensitive area. "You feel incredible," he murmured.

As she began gliding, her gasps and soft cries roared in his ears. He grazed, then pinched her protruding nipples, and she rolled her head back. Once she found a slow, intoxicating rhythm, she continued with her story.

"You whisper in my ear, 'someone is watching us.'" Her insides tightened around him. "But I don't care." She glided faster and raised her arms over her head. "I love the way you feel inside me."

He rubbed her clit and she arched her back, her eyes turning fiery. "Jagger, I...oh, oh...yes. I'm coming." The orgasm ravaged her and she surrendered to the ecstasy.

When the aftershocks stopped, she draped herself over him. He held her tightly and, when she lifted her face to his, he kissed her breathless. "I want you to remember this night for the rest of your life."

Because I'm sure as hell not going to forget this...or her.

5

THE MORNING AFTER

I N THE DIMLY LIT room, Taylor slinked out of bed as soon as Jagger rolled away. She wanted to avoid any awkward "morning-after" conversations or empty promises about getting together. His life—his new life—was out west. She was a realist who lived on the East Coast. Their "no strings" night had been phenomenal and she wanted to remember him in that vein. Even so, melancholy snaked its way around her heart.

It was five forty in the morning. They'd barely had two hours' sleep. As she slipped into her dress, she glimpsed herself in the mirror. Their lust-filled evening flooded her consciousness and her insides clenched with desire. He'd played her body like a virtuoso, until she succumbed to the ecstasy. She'd no idea who this Loving guy was, but she was confident he was trouble.

Though she'd never had a one-night stand, she knew from listening to her girlfriends that this was no ordinary hookup. Playboy or not, the man was a sex god.

Instead of jotting down her phone number, she left her panties on the bed. *A little something from Raven.* She could only find one shoe, so she left it, too. If he found the other, he could donate the pair to a charity.

Before scurrying out, she regarded him one last time. Silky strands of his mussed hair feathered the pillow. She longed to run her fingers over the majestic phoenix inking his broad back. But it was his calm, rhythmic breathing that beckoned. If she didn't escape now, she'd never want to leave him. *Ever.*

She'd had her fun. Time to let him go.

With a heavy heart, she quietly closed the suite door and padded to the elevator in the deserted hallway. Down to the second floor, and then a mad dash to her room.

Once inside, she shed her clothing, unpinned her hair, and headed for the bathroom. After flipping on the faucet, she stepped beneath the spray. Streams of hot water sluiced her tired body while she imagined Jagger's handsome face. Bright eyes that never left hers, chiseled cheekbones, and a strong jaw, covered in a sexy goatee. But his sensual mouth and the passion behind his kisses kept them lip-locked for hours.

As she shampooed her hair, she envisioned his arms holding her tightly and the possessive way he moved inside her. His deep, rumbling laugh. The thickness of his thighs, those bulging biceps, and that light dusting of chest hair. Her insides throbbed with need. *So sexy.* Pretending to be Raven had given her the courage to share her ultimate fantasy, and partake in his. A shudder ran through her. *What if he's married? Oh, god, no.* She vowed not to Google him.

After dressing, she hurried downstairs to check out. She'd taken another day off from work to help Melissa close loose ends with the fundraiser. Though they'd not planned to meet until nine, she didn't want to bump into Jagger in the hotel lobby or restaurant.

In the parking garage, she hurried to her vehicle and stopped cold. The spot where she *thought* she'd parked her car was vacant. She surveyed the area, but her BMW wasn't there. Had she gotten off on the wrong floor? She checked the other parking levels, but her car wasn't on those, either. The magic of her evening vaporized in a puff of panic. What had happened to her vehicle? Rushing back inside, she spoke with the hotel manager.

"I'm very sorry," said the manager. "Several cars were stolen during the night. The police will be here shortly and I'll let you know when they arrive. In the meantime, breakfast is on us."

Seriously? She didn't want food. She wanted her vehicle.

And she did *not* want to run into Jagger.

With no other choice, she waited in the dining room, but she couldn't eat, not with her stomach in knots.

FULL OF ENERGY, JAGGER shot up onto his elbows. Alone in the king bed, he didn't need to check the suite to know she'd bolted. The room felt cold without her. "Dammit."

He dropped back onto his pillow and stared at the beveled ceiling. "Christ, I didn't even get her phone number or her last name." As he pushed out of bed, he glanced at the blank notepad on the night table. *She would have left it, if she were interested.*

Rolling into the bathroom, a headache took root behind his eye. Hoping a scalding shower would drown his frustration, he turned on the faucet and waited for the spray to heat.

While he'd agreed to one night, he'd never had anyone walk out on him. Even at the height of his "nail any attractive woman who crosses my path" phase, he would offer to take her to breakfast in the morning. Playboy, yes, but a cad, no way.

Twenty minutes later, while adjusting his tie in the bathroom mirror, their zesty mirror sex crashed into his thoughts. His chest heated, his dick stirred. Clearly, his body hadn't caught up with the fact that his birthday present had vanished as quickly as she'd materialized.

"Happy birthday." His stern reflection glared back.

He ran his fingers through his damp hair, zipped his Dopp kit, and powered into the bedroom. He'd had no intention of telling Raven it was his birthday, but as he drifted to sleep with her snuggled in his arms, he couldn't wait for breakfast in bed. And a bite to eat after devouring her. Jagger was slow to anger, but there was something about the way she snuck out before dawn that rubbed him the wrong way.

With phone in hand, he replied to a few emails requiring his immediate attention. Everything else could wait. As he grabbed his bags, he spied her pink panties on the bed and her stiletto on the floor. Then, he spotted the other shoe sticking out from beneath the bed. *She'd been in some hurry to leave, hadn't she?* That realization pissed him off even more. He packed the shoes in his overnight bag. Those, he'd donate. Had things been different, he would have returned them to her personally.

He shouldered his bag and strode toward the front door. *Don't leave her panties.* He retraced his steps, grabbed her underwear, and shoved them inside his carry-on. If a photo of those panties— in his suite—ended up on social media, he'd never hear the end of it. *Even I deserve some damn privacy.*

As he rode the elevator downstairs, he considered asking Melissa for Raven's number. But Raven would have jotted it down if she were interested. In reality, their chances of getting together again were slim-to-none. *No strings. No regrets.* The bitter taste in his mouth remained, and the need to see her wouldn't go away.

He entered the hotel lobby and made his way into the restaurant for a breakfast meeting. Even at seven-thirty, the room was buzzing with sleepy-eyed guests.

"Jagger Loving, party of two," he said to the hostess.

"Yes, sir, your guest has arrived. Right this way."

TAYLOR SPOTTED HIM THE second he entered the room. Her heart took off like a thoroughbred when the gate opens. She'd been concerned he'd dine there, and her instincts had been right. She peeked over the top of the Washington Post as Jagger followed the hostess to a table by the window.

A pretty woman rose to greet him. A brief peck on the lips before he held out her chair. Taylor's blood boiled, but she had no business feeling anything toward this man. They'd had an agreement; one that she'd imposed. Still, as he sat facing her, she couldn't help but feel used. *What a player.*

The woman slid a small box across the table. He shot her one of his sexy grins and opened it. Taylor strained to see what looked like sparkling cufflinks.

She should have waited in the lobby, but she couldn't tear herself away. He laughed with ease. His breakfast companion reached across the table to touch his arm. *Why don't you sit on his lap while you're at it?*

The server approached her table. "Ma'am, the police are here. If you're ready, I can escort you."

As Taylor followed the staffer out, she shielded her face with the folded newspaper, but she doubted Jagger would have noticed her anyway. *I told him no strings. I skulked out in the predawn hour. Let it go. I had the best time ever. If anything, Jagger showed me there are men out there who are great in bed. Be happy. Move on.* Though her pep talk helped, her heart ached for that connection. It might have only been one night, but it'd been special enough to question whether walking out on him had been a mistake.

After speaking with the officer, her hope of ever seeing her vehicle again, fizzled. With her stomach in knots, she jumped into a waiting taxi and instructed the driver to take her to Arlington, Virginia. She could have bummed a ride from Melissa, but sticking around was tempting fate.

As expected, the small office space for *Walk a Mile* was dark. She turned on lights, set down her bags, and brewed a pot of coffee in the kitchenette. With a piping hot mug of joe in hand, she powered on the two computers, then called her insurance agency to report the theft. Melissa wasn't due for an hour, so after texting her, she pulled her work laptop from her bag, and got busy. There were always ongoing events to coordinate and manage at Mitus.

Her mind soon wandered back to the auction. She'd overcome a panic attack. Hadn't passed out or fallen flat on her face, either. Those were colossal wins. And then, there was Jagger. His handsome face, that sexy tuft of hair cresting over his brow, and his strong, sculpted physique. She loved the firm way he'd held her, the intensity behind his kisses, and how attentive he was to her needs. She'd never been with a man who cared more about her physical pleasure than his own.

Arousal coursed through her and her cheeks heated. She scurried into the tiny kitchen and yanked a bottle of water from the fridge. Before twisting the lid, she pressed the cold plastic to her forehead. Relief. She was burning with desire.

"Morning!" Melissa exclaimed.

Squealing, Taylor spun around.

"Good God, you'll give me a heart attack. Why are you so jumpy?"

"Not much sleep. My car was stolen."

Melissa's eyes grew wide. "Didn't you park in the hotel garage?"

After Taylor explained what had happened, Melissa offered to pay for the rental car until she could purchase a replacement. "I feel responsible since it happened during the charity event."

"Thank you, but I'd never take *Walk a Mile* funds, plus, my insurance company will cover the cost of a rental. I'm bummed, but it would have been way worse if I'd been carjacked."

"Don't even say those words! I'm so sorry that happened." Melissa smelled the milk before dumping some into her mug.

They left the kitchen and sat at the two desks facing each other in the small workspace.

"So, how was Jagger?" Melissa waggled her brows. "And don't leave out the good stuff."

Taylor leaned over, though no one else was there. "Please don't breathe a word of what I'm about to tell you."

"Of course not. You know I don't gossip."

"He had this sexy tattoo of a phoenix on his back. He was sweet and *great* in bed. My one-night stand was amazing."

Melissa's brows pinched together. "What do you mean, one-night stand? How was he this morning?"

"I left before he woke up. I couldn't bear his disappointment at having to face me after...well, you know. And I didn't want to continue lying to him."

"I'm definitely missing something here." She sipped her coffee. "Why couldn't you just tell him the truth?"

"Absolutely not." Taylor paused to nibble her fingernail. "Being Raven gave me courage to emcee that event, to go upstairs to his suite, to stay there with him, to have sex with a stranger. You know me. I'm terrified of trying anything new. I'm the picture of risk-averse. Raven, on the other hand, was the total opposite, and I never felt so free. I was totally upfront with him and we agreed to a no-strings evening."

"And if he contacts me for your number? Let's keep in mind that he paid for a date with you. For twenty thousand, he deserves an entire week."

They cracked up laughing.

"He lives in California and, from what I could tell, he's super busy. Plus, he's probably forgotten all about me. Those player-types move from one woman to the next."

"You didn't Google him, did you?"

Taylor held up her hand. "No, and I don't want to know anything about Jagger Loving. If he calls you for my number, let me know. I've saved money working at Mitus and will reimburse the charity."

"That's crazy!"

Taylor set down her mug and crossed her arms. "Our paths won't cross again. It was fun—*a lot of fun*—but it's over."

Secretly, she wished it wasn't. She had never met anyone like Jagger Loving and doubted she ever would again.

6

JAGGER'S BIG ASS PROBLEM

J AGGER HUGGED A FRAIL Kimberly Mitus goodbye before exiting the guesthouse on Colton's property. He couldn't leave Virginia without seeing one of his best friends. But his heart broke for Colton and his mother. "I'm sorry," Jagger said to his longtime friend.

"She's a fighter, but she can't beat brain cancer." Colton couldn't hide the sadness in his voice. "Thanks for spending time with her."

In silence, the two men walked towards the main house, a sprawling mansion on Mitus's fifty-acre estate in Great Falls, Virginia.

"I love your mom." Jagger followed Colton into the house. "During college, she was everyone's mother. Is she well enough to travel?"

"Possibly. What did you have in mind?"

"You and Brigit should bring her to my California property. The ocean views offer spectacular sunsets. It might be nice for her. I'd put you up in one of the Presidential suites. Each comes with two private bedrooms."

"Thank you," Colton said as they stepped into the elevator. "I appreciate that."

"I don't know what you're going through," Jagger said. "I only know how I felt when my dad passed away."

Colton's signature nod signaled an end to the discussion about Kimberly Mitus.

They stepped out of the elevator on the main floor, and walked down the long hallway toward the double doors at the end. "Scotch still your favorite?" Colton opened his office door and gestured.

"No alcohol for me, thanks," Jagger said as he entered. "Sparkling or still water is fine." He glanced around the large space. "Great man cave with all the Mitus bells and whistles."

"Thanks," Colton said. "I'm glad you stopped by. It's good to see you."

As Colton poured two sparkling waters, Jagger lifted a framed photo from Colton's desk. "Brigit's beautiful. Maverick said she's perfect for you. Congratulations." Colton's wide grin made Jagger chuckle. "Your smile says it all. Where is she?"

"Her office." Colton tossed another nod toward an open door in the corner before handing the water goblet to Jagger. "I'll grab her when we're finished catching up. I want to hear about your latest resort—especially since I have a stake in it—and the life of an international playboy."

Jagger laughed. "After the incident, I gave up the wild lifestyle. Except for golf, I work like a dog." His phone rang. His assistant was calling. "Gotta grab this."

"I'll check on Brigit." Colton headed toward the corner office.

"Robby, what's the word?"

"We've got a major effing problem. I've had no sleep and I'm freaking out."

Robby operated at a higher frequency than Jagger, but the alarm in his assistant's voice made the hair on the back of his neck prickle. "What's going on?"

"Erin moved to Vegas."

"*What?*" No way would his event director bail at such a critical time.

"She won't return my calls or texts, but she posted a selfie outside a casino with a comment about her exciting, new life," Robby continued. "Her laptop's missing and, from what the event staff told me, she hadn't offloaded much. Beyond the two grand-opening parties, we can't figure out what else has been planned, if anything. We don't know what shows are booked. We've been going nonstop but I have nothing solid to tell you. We are *so* screwed."

With a slow and deliberate move, Jagger set down the glass. "Contact IT and have her passwords killed. HR needs to pull her non-compete. Have them check with legal about taking action against her if they determine she's violated her contract."

"Got it," Robby said. "We open in less than a week! I think I'm going to have a massive coronary."

"Who on the event team could take the lead until we find a replacement?"

"Honestly? No one. David and Adele are good, but they lack the take-charge attitude this exec-level position demands. Ohmygod, I'm having heart palpitations."

"Have you contacted Kate?"

"Your publicist? How can she help?"

"She's well-connected and might know someone we can pull in on short notice."

"Okay...right. I'm in major panic mode. I booked you on an earlier flight, so you need to get to Dulles. I'll text you the flight itinerary and I'll pick you up at LAX."

"Thanks for the update."

"I'm sorry I don't have a solution. Oh, happy birthday, Jagger."

"Thanks." Jagger ended the call. "Dammit."

"What's going on?" Colton asked from across the room.

Refusing to let defeat seep into his bones, Jagger joined him at the window overlooking the back of Colton's expansive property. Jagger had overcome roadblocks and last-minute emergencies before. He'd do it again. But this obstacle was bigger than anything he'd encountered, and he wasn't sure where to start with damage control.

"My event director walked. The staff doesn't know what activities were booked. Robby can't confirm if there's anything besides the daylong cocktail party and the masquerade party, both on opening day. I need one hell of a lot more than that. Jesus, I am so fucked."

A pretty blonde, dressed in a tailored pants suit, entered the room. "Hello, Jagger, I'm Brigit Farnay. Great to meet you."

Jagger forced a smile through the bass drum pounding in his head. "Hello, Brigit." He shook her hand. "It's my pleasure. I hear you've got this guy wrapped pretty tightly."

Laughing, Brigit glanced at her fiancé. "It's mutual."

Instead of being engaged in the conversation, Colton stared out the window, his brow knitted tightly together. "Colton, we've lost you here, buddy."

"Babe, where's Taylor?" Colton asked, raking his hand through his unruly hair.

"Still in Arlington," she replied. "By the way, her car was stolen last night."

Colton powered toward his desk, pressed the speaker button on his phone console, and hit speed dial. While waiting, he shifted his gaze to Jagger. "I might be able to help you."

"Hi, Colton," answered a woman.

Colton lifted the cradle. "Taylor, I'm sorry about your car. Were you in danger?" Silence. "I'm relieved to hear that. Don't rent a vehicle. Use the Prius I leased for my sister. She doesn't need it anymore." More silence. "When are you coming back?" He listened. "Do you need someone to pick you up?" He strummed his fingers on the desk. "I have a special assignment to discuss. We'll talk in the morning," he said, and ended the call.

"Taylor Hathaway is my event planner," Colton said to Jagger. "Her last big project took eight months of prep work. It was that gala I cohosted with Crockett. We raised several million for a non-profit that assists war veterans. She's phenomenal at her job. Since I'm vested in your resort, I'll ask her to help you. If she's willing, I'll put her on the first available flight tomorrow."

"She's smart, easy to work with, and the consummate pro," Brigit added. "You'll love her."

Jagger's headache didn't subside, but a tiny seed of hope took root. He was desperate enough to try anything. "Thank you. My assistant booked me on an earlier flight, so I've gotta bolt. I'm sorry to cut our visit short."

"I'm glad I got to meet you," Brigit said.

"Me, too," he said, hugging her. "If any of my resorts appeal to you guys, your stay is on me. My wedding gift."

Brigit smiled. "That's very generous of you."

"We appreciate that," Colton said.

"Bora Bora is a lover's paradise. Switzerland is breathtaking. Malibu is gorgeous. They're all great places to visit. Google my properties and let me know. Congratulations on your engagement."

"I'll update you as soon as I speak with Taylor," Colton said.

"I hope you call with good news," Jagger replied.

THE FOLLOWING MORNING, TAYLOR knocked on Colton's office door.

"Enter."

She opened the door, stuck her head inside. "You wanted to see me?"

"C'mon in." Colton held out the Prius key. "Car is yours for as long as you need it."

"That's so nice. Thank you." After taking the key, she folded into the guest chair.

Colton strummed his fingers on the desk. "I have a week-long out of town assignment for you."

She perked up. In the four years she'd worked for Colton, she'd never represented Mitus Conglomerate anywhere but the DC area. Plus, getting away would take her mind off...*things.*

"You aren't required to take the job, but I hope you'll consider going," Colton continued. "A close friend is opening a large hotel and his event director bailed. There's nothing scheduled beyond a cocktail party and a masquerade party opening night. It's a lot of pressure and a big task. If you agree to it, I'll extend you an additional week's paid vacation, which you can take immediately following. You'll need the R&R. I doubt you'll get much sleep between now and then."

Shifting in the seat, she nibbled a fingernail. "When would I leave and where is it?"

"Today. The resort is in Malibu."

Be bold. "I'll do it," she blurted, before she could chicken out.

"Thank you, you're a lifesaver." Colton snatched his cell phone and dialed. "Make sure you bring one of your masks. Before you head out, email me outstanding projects so they get handled." With phone to ear, he smiled. "Jagger will be thrilled."

Taylor's brain shorted. *"Who?"*

"Jagger Loving, my good friend and business partner. He stopped by yesterday on his way home and ran into a prob—Hey, Jag, great news. Taylor agreed. I'll text you her flight itinerary. Who'll pick her up?" He listened. "I'll let her know. It's the least I could do for your birthday. Do anything special?" As Colton listened, his grin spread. "Well, you can't beat *that*. Happy belated."

Taylor's blood pressure skyrocketed. *Oh. My. God.*

7

MEET TAYLOR HATHAWAY

As Taylor fastened her seatbelt in first class, she couldn't decide if luck was on her side or if she'd stepped into a black hole of cosmic hell. While she rejoiced at the chance to see Jagger again, ghosting out on him probably hadn't earned her any points. Either way, she had to own the situation. And it sucked.

The airplane accelerated down the runway and she stared out the window. For what seemed like the fiftieth time, she replayed their evening, and the zing of arousal skittered through her. Taylor had never liked her body. But being Raven had bolstered her confidence. Knowing she'd never see Jagger again had freed her to do things she'd only fantasized about. But even if he *had* played her, Jagger Loving had pleasured her in ways she'd never even imagined. For one amazing night, he'd owned her. Body, mind, and soul. And she'd loved every minute of it...until now.

Jagger Loving was her client and that meant one thing. Hands-off.

When the plane went wheels up, she pulled out her laptop. Time to find out about Loving Resorts and the powerhouse of the man behind them.

Each property catered to different clientele. Loving Bora Bora offered the ultimate romantic getaway with private villas in an exotic paradise. No kink events offered, but the promise of a sensually gratifying adventure awaited behind closed doors. Clothing required in public areas. There was a six-month lead time for reservations at this island oasis.

Loving Switzerland was designed with the outdoor enthusiast in mind. This property boasted a little something for everyone. Activities ranged from sweet romance to ultra erotic. In certain areas, like the Jacuzzi room, clothing was optional. This hotel was booked solid eight months in advance. *Holy cow.*

Loving Mexico catered to "the lifestyle". Couples could partake in everything from carnal pleasures with others in the playroom, to workshops that focused on expanding BDSM play. At this resort, nudity was permitted everywhere but the lobby, restaurants and bars. The hotel booked four to eight weeks in advance, depending on the time of year. The more she read about this sexy resort, the more she fidgeted in her seat.

A year ago, Taylor had been tasked with planning an erotic performance event for her boss. Though she'd been a professional planner since college, she'd never booked anything like *that*. Wrought with anxiety, she almost quit. But working with Chastity had been a godsend. The booking manager for sex-play club, Uninhibited, had promised her a quality show and had guided her through the set-up. Taylor simply needed to find out which sexual positions Colton wanted to see. Whether he wanted couples, threesomes, or small groups. Would there be audience participation? What were expectations following the show?

Despite her excellent working relationship with Colton, Taylor communicated via email. She didn't have the nerve to discuss the steamy show in person.

When the big night arrived, Colton had invited his employees, plus a few dozen friends. In order to ensure the program met her boss's needs, she'd monitored the exhibition from the back row... and about died as couples glided and gyrated their way toward orgasms while his guests watched with cool indifference. Deep down, she'd envied the performers' uninhibited nature. Sex for the thirty year old had consisted of the missionary position with the lights out.

Even after that mind-blowing spectacle and the subsequent parties she'd booked, Taylor had remained somewhat of a prude.

Until I—well, Raven—mauled Jagger in his hotel suite.

After typing "Loving Malibu" in the search field, she clicked on the hotel link. Grand opening events included a daylong cocktail party and the Valentine's Day masquerade party that same evening. *That's it?*

She found a brief reference to the club's policy on nudity. Guests could shed their clothing on a secluded section of the private California beach, but that sexy tidbit had been buried several clicks into the site. Taylor chewed the inside of her lip. The Loving sizzle was missing. *Where's the promise of a sensually indulgent vacation?* And this hotel had plenty of available suites, with some of the more expensive rooms being offered at a discounted rate. *Wow, that's not good.*

While Taylor didn't want to discuss *anything* erotic with Jagger, she wouldn't be able to dance her way around the problem. She wiped her clammy palms on the napkin and glanced out the window. *Why is he veering away from his signature branding?*

Armed with enough information to have an intelligent conversation with her new client, she refocused her search on *him*. The first article highlighted his early career. Within three years, he'd fast-tracked his way to the top of a small hotel chain, jumped to a larger one, and then secured an executive position. From what she could find, he wanted to spice up the hospitality landscape. With the help of several investors—one of them being Mitus—he opened his first Loving Resort.

The article read like the typical go-getter workaholic who loved what he did and strove to be top dog. He was well regarded and well respected in the industry, and was an active member of the Hospitality and Lodging Association.

Then, eighteen months ago, when Loving Mexico opened its doors, the articles shifted from Jagger's career to his social life.

Jagger Loving has done it all, seen it all, and pretty much nailed them all. Some women want him for his bucks, others for that rockin' hot bod, but all the ladies can agree about one thing. Loving makes them purr. Eager for a piece of the action, they come from miles around. And from what we've gathered, Loving isn't turning them away.

Her stomach dropped. No strings, no regrets rang hollow in her ears. *He did play me.*

She continued reading. *A year ago, Jagger's life as an international playboy came to a screeching halt when he got caught frolicking with hotel guests.*

Not only had he been blackmailed, but a visit from an ax-wielding husband had forced him to hire a bodyguard. A few months later, the situation had been resolved to everyone's apparent satisfaction and Jagger Loving stopped being front-page fodder for the tabloids. In fact, Jagger Loving disappeared altogether. Until this week, when the press snapped a photo of him talking with a homeless man in DC.

As the plane made its final approach into Los Angeles International Airport, Taylor glanced out the window. Nothing but bright blue sky and a trail of cottony clouds in every direction. But all she saw was red.

Even carefree Raven had been an easy mark for the skilled womanizer. *And I felt badly for walking out on him!*

For the next several days, she'd separate her personal feelings from the job at hand. For all she knew, he'd slept with ten women since bedding her.

Armed with knowledge, she exited the aircraft and, with her head held high, made her way toward baggage claim. Several drivers dressed in black suits and white dress shirts stood in a row, their tablets displaying their clients' names. She spied hers on the tablet of a jittery blond dressed in a light pink shirt, khaki's, and flip-flops. If she wanted, she could breeze right past him, catch a return flight, and tell Colton she wasn't up to the task.

What would Raven do? She wouldn't have thought twice about Jagger after their hookup. Melissa's advice, *make bold choices*, struck a chord. Squaring her shoulders, Taylor set her sights on the slender man, and forged forward.

If Jagger Loving needed an event director, that's exactly what he'd get. Nothing more. Nothing less. Save for the heart palpitations, the sweaty palms, and the churning in her guts, Taylor would bring her A-game.

"I'm Taylor Hathaway. Are you with Loving Resorts?"

"Whew! The angel has arrived to save us from an opening flop! I'm Robby. Robby Sutton, Mr. Loving's assistant." The grinning man pumped the hell out of her hand. She smiled. How could she not? Someone associated with Loving was happy to see her.

"I've got to grab my bag." Taylor plowed toward the luggage carousel with the other passengers.

Robby sent a text. "Letting my boss know I've got you. He's cleared his schedule to spend the afternoon with you." The assistant prattled on and on as suitcases tumbled from the conveyor. Eager passengers grabbed their bags and left.

They waited and waited and waited. The area grew deserted. Two suitcases remained and neither were Taylor's. The nausea she'd been fighting returned with a vengeance. "I'll have to file a claim."

Robby followed her into the small office. The clerk apologized, took her information, and told her they'd call once they'd tracked her suitcase. Besides her carry-on bag filled with bathroom necessities, she had nothing but the clothes on her back. A simple black pants suit and white blouse. Taylor exited the airport with the chatty assistant, and a splitting headache.

Over an hour later, they pulled into Loving Malibu and Taylor's mouth dropped open. Website photos didn't do justice to the magnificent property. Gawking, she hopped out of Robby's vehicle. A seven-story building proudly boasted LOVING on the front. The earth-colored structure reminded her of beautiful adobe-style architecture so prevalent in the southwest. Manicured gardens, with perfectly placed palm trees, dotted the landscape.

She followed Robby inside, but slowed to a stop in the pristine lobby. Everything about Loving catered to the senses. Soothing clay-colored walls created a perfect backdrop against the stark-white furniture. Lush, green foliage in ornate potted planters adorned every available corner, and several vibrant bouquets added bursts of color throughout the elegant space. She had to admit, Jagger had great taste. A crew of workmen lugged paint cans while others carried carpeting or pushed supply carts.

"Right this way." Robby gained speed as he flitted down a hallway. "These are the executive offices." He opened the door at the hallway's end. "Please."

As Taylor crossed the threshold, her fingers tingled with pins and needles while her heart hammered in her chest. Angst replaced confidence. She was about to face the only man she'd hooked up with, and believed she'd never see again.

With his back to her, Jagger sat at his desk, staring out ocean-facing windows. That deep, smooth-as-silk voice rumbled through her. "My event director arrives today." Silence. "Of course I won't talk to the media until you get here." More silence. "I understand your concern, Kate." Phone to ear, he swiveled in the chair, and his cool glance slid from Robby to her.

Recognition flashed across his handsome face. Subtle, yes, but there nonetheless. When a shadow darkened his eyes, a shiver swept through her. She tried to smile, but her lips wouldn't budge.

"I've gotta run." He hung up. With a smoldering gaze, he rose. After fastening the button of his charcoal suit jacket, he offered a smile as stiff as a mannequin's. "Jagger Loving. Welcome, *Taylor.*"

"Taylor Hathaway, Mitus Conglomerate." Though her cheeks flamed, she wouldn't break eye contact. She clutched the back of the guest chair while he seemed to draw immeasurable strength from having home turf advantage. And the fact that he was her client gave him the win. He was in control. She was there to serve him. And she could think of several ways that had nothing whatsoever to do with work.

He extended his hand. She slipped her quivering one into his. Like the first time, the electricity from his firm grip sent a whoosh of energy through her, and that invisible puzzle piece snapped into place. She surveyed his face, his closely trimmed goatee and moustache, and that mouth made for sex. But when their eyes locked, she couldn't deny the effect he had on her.

Total annihilation.

He might be a womanizer, but he had ruined her for any other man. She wanted to hate him for that, but she couldn't.

"The airline lost Taylor's luggage," Robby said, breaking the thick silence.

As Jagger regarded her pants suit, his eyes turned stormy. "Robby, please buy Taylor some clothing in case her luggage never arrives. We can't have our event director running around the hotel nude." His wicked grin wasn't wasted on her.

"Good God, no!" Robby exclaimed. "Should I take her with me?"

"Taylor stays with me." Those four simple words oozed power and control. And so much potential.

"Do you want me to take her on a tour of the property, first?" Robby asked.

As if he had all the time in the world, Jagger stroked his goatee. Back and forth. Up and down. He'd touched her with the same achingly slow pace. In spite of her uneasiness, she couldn't ignore the arousal pounding a line to the small space between her legs. She hated it. She loved it. Either way, she couldn't stop it.

"Later." Jagger hadn't taken his eyes off her since she'd stepped into his office.

Drowning in his intensity, she wanted to cling to the assistant like a buoy.

Robby stepped back and gave her the once-over. "How tall are you? I'm guessing five six or five seven." He glanced at her flats. "Do you wear heels?"

"Stilettos," Jagger answered. "Size eight."

Warmth exploded inside her chest. *He found my shoes.* She didn't trust her own voice, but she had to forge forward. "Yes, I...I wear heels at work. Size eight."

Pausing, Robby eyed them. "Do you two know each other?"

Taylor froze.

"I only ask because," Robby waggled a finger at Jagger, "you seem to know an awful lot about our new—"

"Robby," Jagger interrupted. "Less talking, more action."

"Right." Robby shot Taylor a sheepish smile. "No worries, I'll buy you everything from lingerie to an evening gown, though, nowadays, sexy nighties can be worn as formalwear. Sizes please."

Jagger didn't budge. Taylor had every right to demand privacy and step into the hallway to speak with the assistant. But Jagger had touched her, penetrated her, shared in her fantasy, and confided one of his own. Passing along garment sizes seemed insignificant when compared with all that. So, she rattled them off.

"I'm a runner and would love to take advantage of the California sunshine," she concluded. "I don't know if I'll be able to squeeze in—"

"I've got you covered." Robby finished jotting everything down before shouldering her carry-on bag. "I'll drop this in your suite." After a quick smile, he dashed out.

Alone with Jagger.

A low rumble ripped from the back of his throat, like a growl.

He'd hid his massive ego well the night they'd met, but here, on a Loving property, he was, without question, the one in control and the one with all the power. He exuded confidence. He oozed sex appeal. And she squirmed under his commanding gaze.

The giant wall clock ticked slowly compared to her speeding heart. Should she confess? Should she apologize for not telling him her real name and for vanishing the next morning?

"I'll need your phone number." His words were a command, not a request. "And this time, you're going to give it to me." Damn if he didn't arch his eyebrow at her.

As soon as she did, her phone buzzed.

All thumbs, she fumbled in her handbag, found her phone, and read his text. "Welcome to Loving."

"Thank you, Mr. Loving," she murmured.

When he stepped into her personal space, her breath quickened. She wanted to nuzzle the exposed skin in the V of his white dress shirt. Those damned kissable lips would be the death of her. When she peeked up at him, he was waiting.

"Call me Jagger." His piercing glare cut right through her. "Do you go by Taylor or is there *another* name you'd prefer I use?"

For a long moment, they stared into each other's eyes as the unspoken truth danced on the tip of her tongue.

VERY LITTLE RUFFLED JAGGER, but when Robby returned from the airport with Raven, his mind had stalled. Why had she flown clear across the country to see him when she'd snuck out before dawn yesterday? And what the hell had happened to his new event planner?

And then, reality kicked in. This raven-haired beauty was Taylor Hathaway, sent by Colton. He had a myriad of questions. Why did she leave? Why didn't she jot down her number? Why continue to lie when they were alone, and why in hell had she made up that story about her aunt after he'd told her about being homeless? He'd made a judgment call that this woman was different. But she wasn't. Would he ever learn his lesson? He wanted the damned truth, for once, and then he wanted to ship her back to Virginia.

But his back was against the wall. He needed her expertise to bail him out of an opening disaster. With calculated intensity, he repeated the question. "Do you go by Taylor or is there *another* name you'd prefer I use?"

"What do you want me to say?" she asked, staring into his eyes.

"The truth, this time."

She hesitated, her sapphire eyes stirring up a volcano of need. "Taylor. My name is Taylor."

"Thank you, Taylor. Please, have a seat." Jagger waited until she sat in a guest chair before sitting behind his desk.

He tapped his phone console. "Yes, sir," answered a man. "Has Ms. Hathaway arrived?"

"Yes," Jagger replied. "Coffee and sparkling waters, please, Rico."

"Right away, sir." The line went dead.

Jagger's all-business persona was laced with confidence and a chilly demeanor. On purpose. He wanted her to get the job done and go home. Being played had soured his opinion of her.

As he studied her face, he couldn't deny her sublime beauty. Even her rigid spine and pursed lips didn't detract. But none of that mattered now. "Taylor, I despise deceit, so I'm going to be candid. Obviously, we've met. We had a fun night. Do you have any plans to blackmail me or go public with what happened?"

She crossed her arms, a flash of anger darkening her eyes. "That was personal. I would never—"

He held up his hand, cutting her off. "Good. Let's move on. Did you familiarize yourself with my resort line?"

"Yes."

Time would tell if she were being honest. He leaned back, crossed his legs. "I made poor choices when I lived in Mexico. But thanks to my publicist and my attorney, I'm back on track. This hotel is a reflection of that. It's the opposite of my Mexican resort, on purpose."

A knock on the door interrupted him. "Come in." A server rolled in a cart and set up a fruit tray and beverages on the side credenza. "Thank you, Rico."

"Yes, sir. Good day, ma'am." Rico closed the door on his way out.

Jagger rose. "Coffee? Can I fix you a fruit plate?"

"Just water, please."

He poured her a glass, handed it to her.

Though Taylor smiled, anxiety laced her eyes. His resentment was replaced with a sudden urge to comfort her. Like the evening of the auction, he wanted to wrap her in his arms, then kiss her breathless. The pull he'd felt the night they'd met surged through him.

Hands off. He needed to keep his focus on work, no matter how badly he craved her. If word got out that they'd hooked up, the media would run with that. Didn't matter that they'd had sex *before* she worked for him. She worked for him now.

After filling his mug with coffee, he sat in the second guest chair. To be near her. Because he couldn't stay away.

"My event director bailed, leaving the planning team flying blind," he continued. "Before I introduce you, we need to be on the same page. Instead of being sold out, my hotel is limping along at sixty percent occupancy. That's unheard of for a Loving grand opening. It's no secret that events drive sales, and we need more activities. My guests expect to be pampered, entertained and revered."

"Then you won't take offense at what I'm about to tell you." After setting down the crystal glass, she rested her interlaced fingers in her lap. The atmosphere crackled with undeniable contention, while he waited for her to continue. "You're not sold out because this hotel is like every other one in a hundred-mile radius. The Loving sizzle is missing. There's nothing edgy or sexy happening here. If you're not open to changing things up, I can be out of your hair and on the next flight back to Virginia."

He gritted his teeth. *Well, fuck me.*

8

THE EARTH MOVED

T HIS SITUATION WAS WAY worse than booking a sex event for Mitus Conglomerate because Taylor had never slept with her boss. Discussing *anything* erotic with Jagger felt personal. Despite fidgeting under his scorching gaze, she had to encourage him to bring back the edginess, *and* prove she could be trusted. Rooms wouldn't fill until he offered some spice.

She relocated to his conference table. The furniture gave her much-needed support and put distance between them. Being so close to Jagger interfered with her concentration. She found herself staring at that damned mouth of his.

He joined her, taking his place at the head of the table.

"From what I've read, guests stay at a Loving resort for the sensual experience," she began. "Your other properties are booked months in advance. This hotel is offering discounts to fill beds."

His jaw had been set in a hard line, frustration billowing off him. Her pulse raced. She desperately wanted to change topics and discuss outdoor events like golf and tennis. Those she could handle, no problem.

"What did you have in mind?" he asked, stroking his goatee.

"I need to find out what, if anything, your staff has booked beyond the Valentine's Day masquerade party. We could pull together a G-rated pajama party, along with a Singers & Standards night. For a sexier flair, I'd suggest a lingerie affair. Why not promote the private beach that welcomes nude guests? That would grab their attention."

He pinned her with a hard stare. "And what, offer them sex on the beach?"

Heat exploded on her cheeks. He'd crossed a line. *What would Raven do?* "Look," she stuck out her finger, "I confided something *very* personal and I don't appreciate your throwing that in my face." She'd never confronted anyone like that, and she cringed. "I'm sorry. I was out of line."

His expression softened, but he said nothing for a long moment. "No, Taylor, that's all on me. I apologize." Again, he paused, broke eye contact for a split-second. "I didn't expect...*Raven* would walk through my door." He extended his hand. "Let's start over."

Hearing him call her Raven bolstered her confidence. When she slid her hand into his, the familiar zing of attraction traveled up her arm. "I like that idea."

This time, his smile touched his eyes and her rapid-fire heartbeat slowed back down. "You're right. This resort is nothing like the others. If you read about Loving, you learned about me, too."

"I did."

"I won't do anything that could tarnish my reputation."

"Then you'll really hate what I'm about to say next." She nibbled her fingernail. "You need erotic entertainment."

He grimaced. "Strippers?"

Another rush of heat swept over her and she clutched the table edge for support. "No. Sex performers."

As his long fingers caressed his beard, she fell prisoner to the rhythmic strokes. Her breathing fell in line with his hypnotic touch. Jagger, and everything about him, was proving to be the ultimate distraction.

His harsh grunt snapped her from her fantasy. "Absolutely not." The worry lines around his eyes had deepened.

Beneath the table, her leg bounced. He glanced under and she stilled. "Your brand is all about pushing the envelope," she said.

"Not anymore," he quipped.

Ignoring his objection, she forced herself to continue. Not because she wanted to belabor the point, but because she believed she was offering sound advice. "Time isn't on our side. Since I don't know anything about the erotic market in LA, I can check with a company in DC. They might be able to fly out some talent. Colton can vouch for the professionalism of Uninhibited, but the artists don't hold back. It's definitely edgy."

"Even if I thought it was a good idea, it wouldn't work. We can't offer erotic shows. It's illegal."

"I've got a possible workaround. If guests purchase a membership to a private club that offers the shows to its members, then the hotel should meet the legal requirements for a private club, therefore it's not considered illegal."

He shoved out of the chair, laid his hands on the table, and leaned close. "Not happening." His razor-sharp gaze cut into her.

Although jittery, she rose and faced him. "The rooms will fill, *if* you add the kink back in."

The electricity swirled as the stare-down continued.

"I'll introduce you to your team," he said. "They'll bring you up to speed on event bookings. Do *not* discuss your recommendation with them."

After a confirming nod, she shouldered her handbag. As they walked down the hallway, she snuck in a quick glance. The lingering frustration cast a shadow across his face. His normally bright eyes were dark, his lips slashed in a thin line. Though jittery, she felt empowered that she hadn't backed down.

Jagger introduced Taylor to her staff and left, taking the chill with him. Turning her attention on David Augustine and Adele Shapiro, she wondered how she'd manage through the next several days with a man she wanted to both throttle and throw herself on. He was inciting her last nerve while making her insides hum with desire.

The events team spent the afternoon creating "fun" activities that included a Newlywed game and "chess on the beach" using guests as live pieces. As G-rated events were added to their activities roster, she vowed to change Jagger's mind.

At the end of the workday, Robby zoomed in with a laptop as David and Adele provided Taylor with their cell phone numbers. "Hello, hello!" Like usual, the smiley assistant was bursting with energy.

"Do you want me to use my computer?" Taylor asked.

"No can do," Robby replied. "This has proprietary software you'll need to access for event-planning purposes."

Once Robby had set up her laptop, he ushered her out. "I'm dying to show you what I bought. I've missed my true calling. Personal shopper."

As they rode the elevator to the top floor, Robby explained that the laborers would continue working right up until opening. "The only suites they can't access are on this floor. So, for obvious reasons, you'll be staying upstairs with Jagger and me." He shot her a grin. "Wait until you see the evening gowns I found for you. You are going to look like a princess."

The doors slid open and he escorted her toward one of two Presidential suites. After using the keycard, he opened the door. "Welcome." He handed her the plastic card.

She entered and gasped. The magnificent view of the Pacific Ocean lay beyond the open French doors, and she paused to admire the giant orange fireball sinking into the dark waters.

A beautiful mural of Mayan gods engaging in intercourse had been painted on the living room wall. But the standout piece of hardware was a shiny gold stripper pole in the center of the room.

For the first time since she'd arrived, her headache subsided. *He might not publicly endorse the erotic, but he's still promoting kinky fun behind closed doors.*

Robby escorted her through the living area, stopping in front of a closed door on the far side of the suite. "This is your bedroom. You'll need to use your keycard." She held it against the electronic pad, the light turned green, and Robby shoved open the door.

In addition to her carry-on, the king bed was covered with boutique shopping bags. Three garment bags hung over the bathroom door. "This isn't all for me, is it?"

He waved his hand. "All of it. Like I said, I missed my true calling. Do you think I overbought?"

She laughed. "Uh, yeah."

"I didn't hear from the airline. Did you?"

Taylor shook her head.

"Then, no worries if your luggage never shows. You've got plenty now. If you don't like something or it doesn't fit, let me know."

"I'm sure I'll love everything. You're a total lifesaver. Really, Robby, thank you again for doing this."

He beamed. "You're a sweetheart. I was happy to do it. Hungry?"

"I guess. Jet lag is catching up."

"Food and sleep, in that order. The chef is testing some of his menu items and we're his guinea pigs. You'll love his food. Charles is *amazing.*" Robby headed out.

Dropping her handbag on the bed, she followed, shutting the door behind her. "Will Jagger be joining us?"

"Doubtful. He eats in his office. The man is a machine without an 'off' switch."

Disappointment curled around her heart. On the way through the living room, Taylor spotted a closed door on the opposite side of the spacious suite. "Where does that lead?"

"Jagger's bedroom."

"*What?*" And then she laughed. "You have a great sense of humor."

Robby spun around. "Not joking."

"Why can't I have my own room, downstairs?"

"Like I said, the workmen will be in and out of every room but these two. But if you're uncomfortable in any way—"

"I'm not afraid to be alone with him, if that's what you mean. Why don't you and Jagger share a suite?"

Robby barked out a snort. "If you haven't noticed, I'm a talker. He'd go berserk. Plus, I blare my music non-stop. No headphones. My insomnia keeps me up half the night, so I gab with my friends or play video games. As much as I'd love to have you as my roomie, you'd never get any sleep with me. You're better off staying here."

"Somehow, I doubt that," she mumbled as they proceeded into the hallway.

According to the uber-chatty assistant, Jagger had lured the chef away from a trendy LA restaurant with a hefty starting bonus. Eager to set up his kitchen and prepare the menu, Charles Delateau had been working there for a few days.

The beefy man greeted them with a boisterous hello and a friendly smile before ordering them to sit at the chef's table in the kitchen, where two bottles of wine—a Pinot Blanc and a Sémillon —awaited. Taylor envied his speed and grace as he moved about the workspace.

"Tonight, you'll sample petite portions of several entrées," Charles explained. "I'm incorporating favorites dishes with a few new ones that pair well with the season." Pausing at the table, he wiped his hands on his apron. "Tell me about allergies and food restrictions, like gluten or red meat."

"No allergies, but I won't eat rice pudding," Taylor said with a playful grin.

Charles laughed. "Okay. Fair enough. Robby?"

"I'm allergic to peanuts and shellfish."

"Hmm. Stay clear of my fish appetizers. Often times, I'll mix in lobster with my salmon."

"What happens to you?" Taylor asked.

"I blow up like a puffer fish." Robby demonstrated by pushing air into his cheeks. "Seriously, though, I've had some bad reactions and carry an EpiPen." He shrugged. "It's upstairs."

"Tonight's meats are chicken and salmon." Charles returned to his station. "I'll forgo the shrimp."

After a delicious meal, Taylor acknowledged that jet lag had won and excused herself. She hoped she'd find Jagger in the suite. Though wrong, she wanted to see him in the absolute worst way.

But the suite was quiet, and loneliness settled over her.

The constant pull to be near him made her heart ache. She'd left the French doors open, and though the room was chilly, the ocean breeze felt balmy when compared with the freezing DC temps.

She stood on the balcony, salty air filling her lungs. The crescent moon cast little light on the ocean, but the rolling waves soothed her anxious soul. She closed her eyes and breathed. Seconds later, Jagger crashed into her thoughts, pulled her into his arms, and kissed her. Her soft groan startled her and she opened her eyes. But she remained alone on the quiet balcony, the constant yearning her sole companion.

Even if she hadn't met him at the auction, she'd be crazy attracted to him. Beyond his striking looks, he carried himself with a worldly sophistication she could only dream about. He was confident without being cocky, and simmering with a sexy, unassuming charm.

But she'd never slept with a client or a coworker, and she wasn't about to start now, no matter how strong the pull. In the four years she'd worked at Mitus, she'd never dated anyone on Colton's staff. No man had moved past the "friend" stage. But Jagger was different, and she struggled to reconcile her feelings.

Ten o'clock West Coast time was no match for her tired eyes and aching muscles. Her East Coast brain screamed one in the morning. After a relaxing shower, she peeked into the shopping bags before lining them up on the floor next to the mirrored wall. Everything Robby had purchased was both stunning and elegant.

She slipped under the linens, turned out the bedside lamp, and dropped her head on the fluffy pillow. Burrowing beneath the cozy sheets, she closed her eyes. She'd survived day one of Jagger Loving and his kink-free resort. *Hopefully, tomorrow I'll have better results.*

Exhaustion set in. As she drifted to sleep, she imagined her absentee suitemate holding her tightly and loving her all night long.

SHE AWOKE WITH A start, confused. *Who's running the disposal?* The bed vibrated and the room swayed. The alarm clock danced on the nightstand. *Earthquake!*

On a screech, she bolted out of bed and charged into the living area. The table lamp flickered as the door to Jagger's bedroom flew open and he strode out. Crashing into him, she threw her arms around him. Trembling, she eked out, "Er-er-er-earthquake?"

"Yes. I've got you." His steady voice calmed her as he whisked them into his room and positioned them in the doorway of his bathroom, quickly flipping on the light.

Just as suddenly as the rumbling had started, it stopped. Silence, save for her erratic breathing, thundered in her ears.

Taylor startled when Jagger's cell phone and the cordless wall phone in the bathroom began ringing. With one arm anchored around her waist, he snatched the receiver with his other hand. "Loving."

And that's when she realized they were both stark naked.

Instead of pushing away, she clung tighter, his warm, hard body exciting her in a myriad of ways.

"I'm fine, Robby. You okay?" A pause. "She's with me," he said, regarding Taylor. "Call the building inspector." He hung up and, with her still nestled in his arms, answered his cell. "Loving." He listened. "That's good news. Keep me posted and thanks for the call." He hung up and tossed his cell phone onto the king bed.

"Are you okay?" His business tone had been replaced with a huskiness that weakened her defenses.

Though still quivering, she needed to break away. But she couldn't. Being in his arms felt safe and exciting and right. Which was so incredibly wrong.

The atmosphere turned electric. His breath hitched, his bright eyes bled black with desire. She couldn't steady her breathing or halt her trembling. The fear from the quake had morphed into a tsunami of desire.

A hungry, raspy moan ripped from her throat.

"Dammit, Taylor." His mouth found hers. The deliciousness of his sexy sounds exploded through her, shattering her defenses.

Again, the bathroom phone rang. He softened the ravenous kiss, dropping tender pecks on her mouth. When he plucked the receiver, he didn't let her go.

"What did you learn?" While listening, he pressed his lips to her forehead. She melted from the tenderness. Though Robby talked nonstop, her focus remained on Jagger.

She loved how they clung to each other, though the immediate danger had passed. His strong, steady breathing and his deep, controlled voice soothed her. The earth had shifted, the building had swayed, but not Jagger. She wanted him, but the need went beyond the physical. He was everything she was not. Calm. Steady. In control. And that affected her in the best of ways. In his embrace, she had stopped shaking. Relieved, she inhaled a breath. And his delicious baseline scent reminded her of the most exciting night of her life.

"Good work, Robby. Thanks for checking the exterior doors."
He listened. "Of course, I'll assure her. See you in the morning."

He hung up, and wrapped her in his arms. Heat blossomed in
her chest while she gazed into his eyes.

"Robby suggested I keep you company in case there are
aftershocks. And I have a feeling there will be *plenty*."

Adrenaline shot through her. "Jagger, we shouldn't. You're my
client." She despised the words as they spilled from her.

"Have you thought about me at all since our night together? Be
honest with me, Taylor."

Spurred by her need to be truthful, she found her voice. "Yes, I
have. What about you?"

A shadow darkened his bright eyes. "The question is: When
haven't I thought about you?"

"You want Raven," she whispered, crestfallen.

He kissed her gently. "I want the woman I met at the auction.
Bold one moment, timid the next. Gorgeous, somewhat unsure,
and totally hot."

She was fighting the desire to be with him...and losing. He
kissed her shoulder, his lips lingering on her heated skin.

"I want to feel you beneath me," he murmured. "Touch every
inch of your beautiful body. But more than that, I want to make
you scream my name from the pleasure I can bring you. None of
that matters, though, if that's not what *you* want."

Make bold choices. "I do want you, Jagger." She launched herself
onto him. Her kiss was brutal. Hungry mouths and crushing
tongues. She fisted his hair with one hand and raked his back with
the fingernails of her other, her erratic breathing interrupted by
her desperate moans.

His kisses tormented her. Soft and tender one moment. Hard
and unrelenting the next. She opened her eyes. He slowed the kiss,
then ended it, but wouldn't let her go.

"Do you feel this?" he murmured.

She smiled. "I feel *something*."

His low, deep chuckle rumbled through her chest to her heart. "Not that. Us. This is more than passion or sex. This is...*real*." He stopped as if surprised by his own words. "You're elegant, lovely, the whole package."

He turned her around so she faced the mirrored wall, and wrapped his arm across her chest, anchoring his hand on her shoulder. His gaze roamed with ease over her nude body.

The weight of self-consciousness bore down on her. Her youth had been filled with taunting about her skinny legs and flat chest. She slammed her eyes shut against the whoosh of painful memories.

"You're so damned beautiful." He leaned around, kissing her cheek.

Shivering from vulnerability, she refused to look at her reflection. "I can't watch me."

With a tenderness that tugged at her heart, he turned her toward him. "I'm sorry. I didn't know this makes you uncomfortable. Why didn't you tell me the first time?"

"Raven was fearless."

As he studied her, she flushed. "I see."

"If I'm being completely honest, I don't like looking at myself in the mirror. All I see is everything that's ugly or wrong. But I liked having mirror sex with you. A lot. I'd never done anything so sensual."

A brief smile relaxed the etched worry lines between his brows. "I like you honest, Taylor." He kissed her. "My turn to be truthful. I want you. I want to make love to you. But I don't want you skipping out on me again."

"You're a playboy and—"

"Not anymore," he said, cutting her off. "I've had two dates in the past year. Slept with one of the women, *once*. I'm breaking every damned rule with you. Because there *are* no rules when I'm around you. You hold all the power."

"I want to try the mirror again."

"Not if it makes you uncomfortable."

"Is that the only way you like to...um, you know?"

"No, it's not." He pecked her cheek. "Reflection sex gives us a different perspective. Together, we see how we connect, how we react to each other's touch. All of you becomes my entire universe and that excites me."

Try. "If I stay focused on you, I can do this." She shot him a tiny smile. "That worked great the first time."

His eyes flashed with excitement. "I have an idea. Did you bring your mask for the masquerade party?"

"Uh-huh, but it's in my lost luggage."

"Wear mine."

Her chest tightened. "You want Raven."

"No, I don't, but *you* seem to need her."

He's right. After allowing him to tie his mask on her, she glimpsed herself in the mirror. Even masked, her insecurities came racing back and she fastened her gaze on him.

He resumed his place behind her, snaked his arm around her waist, and pulled her flush against him. "I see beauty and strength."

His deep timbre, paired with the sincerity in his eyes, had the most calming effect on her. Was Jagger the right person to help her conquer her long-term insecurity? As they stared into each other's eyes, the air sizzled with electricity. He regarded her with a hunger that made her breath hitch and her heart beat quicker. Though uncomfortable, she shifted her attention to her reflection. "This is really difficult for me."

"Close your eyes."

When she did, he kissed her shoulder, stroked her breast, teased her nipple with his fingertip. Each time he touched her, she needed more. The intensity with which she craved him scared her. She could get so lost in this man.

When he ran his fingertips across her stomach, she giggled, and her eyes popped open.

"You're ticklish," he said, smiling. "How are you doing?"

"I love your touch."

"Are you okay, Taylor?"

"Yes. I feel safe with you."

"Good," he murmured in her ear as he fondled her breasts. "Can you watch what I'm doing? Your nipples are so responsive."

With one arm draped over her chest, clutching her shoulder, his other hand played her like an instrument. It was as if he knew her better than she knew herself. He nuzzled her neck until he found the spot just before her shoulder that made her whimper. His raspy, needy growl rumbled through her, and she gripped his arm for support.

She shifted her attention and, like always, wished for larger breasts.

"Touch yourself." He guided her hand to her breast, and she squeezed her swollen nipple. "Your breasts are beautiful, like you."

Then, he covered her other hand with his, and guided her over her abdomen and around to her bottom. "This is one hot ass. I hope you know that."

Smiling, she leaned around to kiss him. His groan ripped through her as he continued exploring her body. With interlaced fingers, he guided them over her hip and down to her core. Arousal hijacked her thoughts when he slipped their fingers between her folds.

"Oh, so good," she murmured.

"I love how wet you are for me."

She hadn't realized she'd continued massaging her breast and pinching her nipple until he murmured, "My God, you're gorgeous."

As she watched them in the mirror, his breathing quickened, his hardness pressing against her backside. Arousal coursed through her and she raised her arm over her head and sank her fingers into his hair. Now, completely open to him, she began to gyrate against him.

And then, he penetrated her with his finger and she choked out a strangled cry. "You...oh, Jagger...mygod." Her eyes fluttered closed.

"Taylor, look at us."

She opened her eyes, captive in his embrace.

"What do you see?" he asked.

"Everything that's wrong. My limbs are too thin, my breasts are too small." She stopped moving. "This won't work."

"Do you know what I see?" he murmured before kissing her temple. "I see a goddess. Let Raven see what Taylor cannot."

Though she struggled with his words, she peeked at her reflection.

He caressed her breast and squeezed her engorged nipple between his thumb and forefinger. She whimpered from the shock of pain mixed with a heady euphoria. His mouth lingered on her shoulder with a kiss that made her knees go weak. When he pressed his hand against her abdomen, he skewered her with a hungry gaze, and she trembled from his intensity.

Slowly, he moved his hand to her swollen clit. A raspy groan shot from the back of her throat and she started moving against him. Everything about him made her want to push beyond her insecurity.

"You are perfect exactly the way you are," he rasped. "I could stare at you for hours and still want more."

No man had ever made her feel this way. Empowered by his encouraging words, she peered at herself in the mirror. His hands never stopped moving over her. His deep, sexy groans undid her, but when he pressed his mouth against the nape of her neck, she surrendered to the ecstasy. Unable to stop herself, she cried out. Hard, violent convulsions shredded her as she watched herself come in the mirror.

Slowly, the spasms subsided and she relaxed against him. When she gazed into his eyes, love stared back. Assuming this outburst of emotion stemmed from the orgasm, she rejected the feeling outright. "Thank you," she murmured.

"Thank you for trusting me," he replied.

"Do you need me masked?"

"No, that was for you."

She bowed her head. He untied and removed the mask. She turned to face him and he wrapped her in his arms, kissing her until she gasped for air and moaned for more.

"I need you," she said. "Inside me."

"I have one condom left from our three-pack." His lazy grin slayed her.

"I didn't know 'we' had a three-pack." She threaded her fingers through his and led him into his bathroom. After a quick search in his Dopp kit, she found the condom.

An aftershock rumbled through the room and she flung her arms around him. He pulled her flush against him and kissed her. In seconds, the tremor subsided. "The upside to these quakes is you, in my arms."

Smiling, she kissed him. "Maybe your braveness will rub off on me." Tugging him into the bedroom, she stopped next to the bed. "Where do you want me?" she asked. "Mirror?"

"I want you beneath me," he said. "And then I want you next to me, all night long."

She melted. Jagger had this way of making her feel like she was the only person in the world, and the only woman who mattered.

HE COULDN'T STOP KISSING her face, her neck, and each breast. He couldn't get enough of this amazing woman. But when she levered her hips, he drove himself inside her. And she came alive beneath him. Clawing his back and biting his lips. Her raspy coos sent a rush of heat straight to his throbbing cock.

He tugged her nipples with his teeth and suckled the plumped nibs. "I love the way you do that," she murmured. "That's so sexy and ohmygod, that makes me crazy."

"I want to slow down, appreciate how good you feel beneath me."

"I'm so close. I need a release." She cemented her hands on his ass and forced him in deeper. She grunted out a series of throaty moans, her sexy sounds echoing in his ears.

He didn't want to come. Not yet. But she raised her arms onto the pillow and commanded, "Hold me down."

When he clasped her wrists, she wrapped her legs around his back. And he was powerless to stop the onslaught of pleasure. "Taylor, I'm going to come."

She arched toward him and he sunk in deeper, the orgasm teetering on the brink. "Look at me."

Taylor's sexy command sent him careening over the edge, but it was her ocean-blue eyes that seeped into his soul. Nothing timid about the woman writhing beneath him. Nothing timid at all.

He waited until he could catch his breath. Then, still nestled inside her, he rolled them over, so she was on top. "Wow, you're a wild thing."

She kissed him. Deep, full of passion, and sexy as hell. When she ended the embrace, her sated smile let him know he'd done right by her. And he smiled in return.

Leaning up on her elbow, she combed her fingers through his hair. Her soft touch soothed him in ways he'd never imagined. After tucking her hair behind her ear, he kissed her, again and again.

"When I look in the mirror, I see everything I don't like," she said, her voice hushed. "You make me feel beautiful and sexy."

"You *are* beautiful." He framed her face in his hands and dropped a soft kiss on her mouth. "Damned sexy with a killer body, too." Her cute smile landed in his heart. "I need two minutes in the bathroom. If you're not here when I come out, I'm going to break down the door to get to you." He flipped her over, kissed the hell out of her, and pushed out of bed.

He returned to find her sitting up in bed, dressed in a hotel robe. She'd propped up his pillows and had folded back the linens.

"Hi." She patted the mattress.

"Hello, gorgeous," he said as he relaxed onto the pillows.

After covering his legs with the linens, she said, "I want to understand why there's no kink at this resort."

"No shop talk." Beneath the linens, he stroked her bare thigh.

"This is important."

"My mistakes aren't up for discussion."

"And I'm a total mess in front of a mirror while you encourage me to watch us. There are no words for how difficult that is for me."

"You're comparing two completely different things." Frustration tinged his words.

"I'm so insecure about my body that I had to put on a mask and pretend to be someone else." Pausing, she bowed her head. "And I'm not sexually experienced, either. It would be much easier if I continued booking fun events and never discussed the kink. But I'd be ignoring the real issue. Playing it safe isn't working."

Silence.

A throbbing in his temple replaced the lingering pleasure. He did *not* want to discuss his life and the choices he'd made.

She turned toward him, pulled her knees to her chest, and caressed his chest. Her tenderness slowed his hammering heart. Then, she shot him a sweet smile of encouragement. "Please trust me."

Trust did not come easily to Jagger. "If you want me to trust you, let's start with the truth."

"Okay."

The sincerity in her eyes urged him forward. "When we were alone at the hotel, why didn't you tell me your real name?"

"I would never have had the courage to stay with you." Her

cheeks flushed with color. "Being Raven empowered me. I'm sorry I told you I was a vet."

He acknowledged her with a nod. "I confided that my family was homeless. Why the story about your aunt dying on the streets?"

Sadness bled from her eyes. "I *was* being honest about that, Jagger. My Auntie Patty did live with us throughout my childhood and she died homeless. It wrecked me."

Forgiveness washed over him as he peered into her eyes. "I'm sorry for your loss." Now, he could move forward. But should he?

"Please," she murmured.

His guts churned while his pulse raced. Desperate to escape his past, he shoved out of bed, opened the French doors, and inhaled the crisp nighttime air. *Tell her.* Another pause before he turned to face her. "My mistakes almost cost me *everything.*"

"Push past your fear like I'm pushing past mine," she encouraged. A kaleidoscope of emotions filled her face. "Help me understand what's driving this change." She folded her hands in her lap and waited.

Regarding her, he pondered his options. Could he trust her with the *entire* truth?

"I paid my publicist and my attorney a *lot* of money to clean up my mess and restore my reputation. I've got my life back. I'm not doing anything to jeopardize that."

"Jagger, is the kink too tempting?"

"No." In order for her to fully understand, he had to tell her everything. Another moment passed. *Go on.* "I was on a destructive path. I forgot who I was, where I came from."

"What about your other resorts?"

"I'm in conversations to sell those."

"I see," she said, her brow furrowed. "Is that what *you* want to do?"

"It's what's best."

"I don't und—"

"Ever been homeless?" he asked, cutting her off.

She shook her head.

Chills shot down his spine. He hated remembering this part of his life. "Ever watch your mom give up food so her kids could eat?"

Sad blue eyes blinked up at him. "No."

"We got kicked out of our cramped apartment. I saw my mom's pain and anger when she realized my dad had been feeding his drug addiction with rent money."

After a pregnant pause, she whispered, "I'm sorry."

"I appreciate your dedication to *Walk a Mile* but until you *actually* walk in my shoes, don't assume you know the fears that drive me." A stabbing pain pummeled his chest.

"Okay," she whispered.

Tell her. "The sex photos that went viral were designed to grab my attention. The real issue was the pictures and videos of me popping pills and snorting massive amounts of coke. The women wanted millions to keep quiet." Ashamed, he turned away. "I'd become a hard-core drug addict. Even started selling to my guests. Not for the money, but to surround myself with a steady stream of dealers providing me with the strongest drugs on the market. My life revolved around my next high and I put my business and my reputation at risk. When key executives confronted me, I threatened to fire them. I grew ugly and hated myself, but I couldn't stop."

She flew out of bed and into his arms. "Jagger, I'm sorry."

He kissed her with an intensity that scared him.

"Thank you for confiding in me," she murmured.

"I got clean and sober." His throat tightened, the emotion threatening to explode out of him. "No way in hell would I end up like my father."

"The phoenix rising from the ashes." She leaned up to kiss his cheek. "You should be proud of what you've overcome."

He cradled her face in his hands. "Only my attorney and my

publicist know the full extent of my problem. Not even my closest friends realized how bad things got. Hitting rock bottom was one hell of a wake up call."

He hugged her tightly. Goddamn it to hell, it was scary, but it felt amazing. For the first time in his life, he'd let someone in who wasn't being paid to keep quiet and clean up his mess.

Jagger had experienced everything but the true love of a good woman. As she shed her bathrobe and they crawled into bed, he wondered whether this amazing woman could be the one.

9

THE SHIFT

A S TAYLOR LISTENED TO her team discuss the laundry list of activities, her mind strayed. Even curled in Jagger's arms, she hadn't slept well. Her heart felt heavy. Fear was preventing him from embracing the brand that had made him a success. She doubted the hotel would sell out, even with the in-house spa and the entertainment. There were too many other five-star properties in the vicinity competing for market share.

Though he'd invited her for an early morning run, she'd declined. Being seen outside of a work-related event might catch the eye of a photographer. With his publicist arriving that morning for media day, the paparazzi would be hungry for a shot of Jagger.

"*Taylor*," Adele said. "What do you think?"

"I'm sorry, what did you say?"

"Do you like our suggestions for additional events?" David asked. "Can we move forward with Surfing 101? What about parasailing? And we'd like to arrange for offsite wine tours, too."

Taylor slid her focus from one to the other. "They all sound great." But they didn't. Not when she knew what they *could* be offering.

Knock. Knock.

Jagger walked in, his sights set on Taylor. "How's it going?"

"Good," Taylor replied. "What can we help with?"

"My publicist is here. Can I steal you for a few?"

"Of course." After asking her staff to follow through on their suggestions, she left her office.

"You look beautiful," he said as they headed down the hall.

Before she could respond, she walked into his office and her brain stuttered. There stood Kathy Jones, the last person Taylor expected—or wanted—to see. *Oh, God, no.* Jagger's publicist was the she-devil herself. Other than the couture suit, Kathy hadn't changed. Same highlighted ringlets dangling on her shoulders, same shade of power-red lipstick, and same oversized black-framed glasses framing those cold, unblinking eyes. But it was Kathy's haughty expression that made Taylor's skin crawl.

"Taylor!" Squeezing Taylor's shoulders, Kathy air-kissed each cheek. "Mmmwa. Mmmwa Big kisses. Small world."

Jagger gestured toward his conference table. "Let's sit."

Brushing past, Kathy claimed the chair at the head. Taylor crumpled into the seat across from Jagger, resigned at having to work with this two-faced witch.

"How do you two know each other?" Jagger asked.

"She knows me as Kathy Jones," Kate answered. "We were close friends in high school—" Kathy cocked her head—"and sorority sisters in college."

"You two can catch up later," Jagger said. "We've got a packed—"

"When I got married," Kate flashed her wedding band, "I changed my last name. Kathy Faraday had no pizzazz. I toyed with using my real name, Kathryn, but ultimately decided on Kate. Kate Faraday sounds regal, doesn't it?" Her arrogant tone made Taylor's blood run cold.

With a curt nod, Jagger shifted his attention to Taylor. "Run through your scheduled events so we're all on the same page."

Ignoring Jagger, Kate continued. "Tell me about you, Taylor." After eyeing Taylor's ring finger, Kate frowned. "Not married, poor baby. So, you're an organizer. That's perfect for you. Your locker and dorm room were always super tidy."

Kathy Jones still excelled in controlling the situation while sucking the life force out of everyone in her self-serving path.

As Taylor's stomach roiled, she addressed Jagger. "I'll begin with opening-day events—"

"Email those to Jagger and me," Kate said, her flinty voice grating on Taylor. "We need to focus on media day. Jagger and I will field all questions. Immediately following, I'll schedule a series of mini interviews. Ten minutes, tops." She flicked her head toward Taylor, sending the tight curls flying. "I'll ask one of the local rags to interview our very own event coordinator."

"*Kate.*" Jagger's commanding tone hijacked their attention. "Make no mistake, Taylor is part of my executive team."

She wanted to hug him for defending her, but she said nothing.

"I've made an important decision you both need to hear before I speak with the media." Jagger's confident posture, paired with that deep timbre, soothed Taylor's jitters.

Leaning forward, Kate said, "I'm all ears."

Robby barreled into the room wheeling Taylor's lost suitcase. "Ta-da! Look what just got delivered."

"That's great," Taylor exclaimed.

"Good to see you, Kate," Robby said. "You're fab, as always."

When Kate beamed, Taylor glimpsed her porcelain veneers. "I do my best."

"The media are congregating in the lobby," Robby said. "What should I tell them?"

Kate rose. "Say nothing. I'll handle this."

"Taylor, do you want me to run your suitcase up to your suite?" Robby asked.

"I can do it," she replied.

"I'll go with you." Jagger pushed out of the chair. "I want to change into a suit."

"Are you two on the same floor?" Kate asked.

"We're sharing one of the Presidential suites," Jagger replied. "Separate bedrooms."

As Kate glared at Jagger, her jaw ticked. "Ohmygod, Jagger. Please tell me you aren't…" Grunting, she folded her arms. "I worked my ass off cleaning up your reputation. Why doesn't Taylor have her own suite?"

"Relax, Kate. You're making something out of nothing."

"Am I?" Kate shot him the death stare. "Robby, where are you staying?"

"In the suite next door."

"Robby, you move in with Jagger. Taylor and I will share. That will give us some girl-time to catch up."

"Kate—" Jagger said.

She dismissed him with a wave of her hand. "I'll be in the lobby. Robby, do you have the podium and mic set up?" She left before he could answer, and he zoomed out after her.

Sharing a suite with Kate was the last thing Taylor wanted to do.

Across the table, Jagger regarded her with a glint in his eyes. The atmosphere turned electric, and thoughts of having to work with Kate faded. Frustration morphed into desire.

"I'll sneak you into my room in the middle of the night." His playful grin made her smile.

Inasmuch as she liked that idea, she had to put a stop to their hooking up. "We can't. Kathy…*Kate* has a point. I don't want to do anything to hurt your reputation." She stood and, gripping her suitcase handle, she headed out.

He was by her side, his hand on her shoulder, pulling her to a stop. His possessive touch both soothed and aroused her.

"Don't let what she said drive a wedge between us." He edged closer, but she stepped away, leaving a respectable distance between them. "I'm making an announcement and I want you by my side when I tell the media."

FOR THE FIRST TIME in a long while, Jagger felt solid and whole. The risk he was about to take was the right one. For the past nine months, he'd been playing things safe. Laying low and letting the press chew on other stories. His rehab had gone well. He didn't miss the booze, and he'd stopped the self-loathing for doing drugs. Though he'd known better, one bad decision had snowballed into a hellish nightmare from which he could barely escape.

He didn't miss the whoring around, either. But he had missed the warmth of a woman. Not just the sexual heat, but the connection between two people who thoroughly enjoyed each other's company.

Then, in walked Raven. Sexy, dynamic, carefree. But the sweet, surprisingly determined, Taylor Hathaway had stolen his heart.

He'd woken up in the middle of the night and watched her sleep. Beyond the obvious beauty, her unassuming nature had touched him. He didn't understand why she disliked her body, but he wouldn't dismiss her feelings simply because *he* found her sexy. If she were willing to step outside her comfort zone and trust him sexually, he would step outside his and trust her professionally.

After changing into a charcoal suit, crisp white shirt, and power-red tie, he returned to the lobby alone, on purpose. When he finished shaking the hands of the business leaders and government officials, along with greeting the journalists, he made his way to the podium.

His executive team stood behind the speaker's stand. One by

one, he shook each of their hands while the media documented his every action.

When he stopped in front of Taylor, her sapphire blue eyes bore into his. Though she shook his hand like a consummate pro, her loving touch reaffirmed his decision. She wasn't just his event director—she was his angel. As he peered into her eyes, he said, "Thank you for believing in me."

Her sweet smile empowered him. He was making the absolute right choice.

He walked to the podium, adjusted the mic, and smiled at the crowd. Though Kate had advised him to avoid the topic that had been his downfall, he would address it, starting right now.

"Welcome to Loving Malibu," Jagger began. "I'm extremely proud of our first American-based property and we are honored that the beautiful, majestic state of California has welcomed me home."

After introducing his team, Jagger paused. *Confront the past. Embrace the future.*

He cleared his throat. "The past year has been a sobering one for me." The audience chuckled politely. "I regret my choices in Mexico, but learned a great deal from them. What you don't know is that I'm a recovering drug addict."

The clicking of cameras stopped. Scribbling reporters stilled their pens.

"My habit started with recreational cocaine. A snort or two to clear the cobwebs from the previous night's hangover. Things progressed until life revolved around my addiction and spiraled out of control."

He inhaled a sobering breath.

"After hitting rock bottom, I dropped off the grid. Then, I checked into a fantastic facility to begin the slow climb out. Today, I'm proud to be clean and sober. I don't miss the burn of whiskey or the full-bodied taste of a 2000 Latour Bordeaux, and I sure as hell don't miss the drugs. I'm grateful for my sobriety, one day at a time."

Damn, speaking the truth feels great.

"Enough said. Let's move on."

He highlighted several activities designed to indulge and pamper his guests. Reporters resumed note taking, while others held up their phones to record his speech.

"I'm sure you've noticed the erotic element so prevalent at my other properties is missing from this one. That was a calculated move as a gesture that I'd cleaned up my act." Jagger grinned. "My act is so clean, it squeaks."

Several in the audience chuckled.

"My previous event director didn't work out, but one of my investors, Colton Mitus of Mitus Conglomerate, asked his event planner to step in and bail me out." He turned toward Taylor. "Taylor Hathaway, please join me."

Her cheeks flushed. She didn't move. He addressed the audience. "Let's give Taylor some encouragement."

As Taylor took her place beside him, the room filled with light applause. Though she smiled, her body stiffened. He wanted to place a reassuring hand on her shoulder, but any physical contact would give him away.

"Loving Resorts book out months in advance. As much as it pains me to admit, Loving Malibu is nowhere near full capacity. The loss of potential business doesn't just affect my hotel, it's bad for local businesses, too. Under Taylor's advisement, I'm spicing things up by adding kink back onto the menu."

Again, the room quieted and the flash of cameras stopped.

"Taylor, please share some of the details."

Kate bolted to the podium and yanked the built-in mic toward her. "Hello, everyone. Kate Faraday, Mr. Loving's publicist. I'm afraid we're out of time. Mr. Loving and I will be conducting interviews after lunch. Please, head on over to the restaurant and we'll see you shortly." She snapped off the mic and, though she smiled at Jagger, her pulse throbbed in her temples.

"We need to talk," she said through clenched teeth. "Now." She shot Taylor a passing glance. "Alone."

"There's nothing to discuss, Kate."

"We had an agreement," Kate replied. "I deserve to be brought into the loop on a major decision like this." She marched toward Jagger's office.

"Join us," Jagger said to Taylor.

Once the three were secluded in his office, he closed the door.

"What the hell was that?" Kate demanded, hand on hip.

"That was me returning to my core brand," Jagger replied. "And I've got to tell you, it feels fantastic!"

"Kathy—" Taylor said.

"It's *Kate*." She glared at Taylor. "You're an event planner. Period. You don't know market strategy. You haven't been with him. You can't begin to understand the mess he made of his life. I'm the reason he's back on his feet."

"No, Kate, you're not." Jagger slipped a hand into his pants. "I confronted my demons and my past. I did the work and I am no longer that man."

"You say that *now*!" Kate's face reddened. "Wait until some tits and ass cross your path. Or you pop a cork on a champagne bottle. And don't get me started about *everything* else. Whatever the temptation, you'll go right back to snorting and screw—"

"*Enough*." Jagger lowered his voice, widened his stance. "Do not talk to me like I'm a child. *You* work for *me*. The fun events and sweet romance will outweigh the erotic, but Taylor is right. It's my core brand and it stays."

Kate whirled toward Taylor. "You're a dear friend, but you don't know the first thing about kink."

Like hell she doesn't. Jagger bit back a smile.

"I'll be in my office," Taylor said, ignoring Kate. "What's my budget?"

Jagger tossed her a nod. "Whatever it takes."

TAYLOR CLOSED HER OFFICE door and hugged herself to quell the shakes. Under the circumstances, she'd held up pretty well. Kathy Jones had walked all over her in high school and again, in college. No matter how much she loathed confrontation, she couldn't allow Kate to dictate what would be in Jagger's best interest.

With no time to spare, she called the booking manager at DC's members-only sex-play club, Uninhibited.

"Hey, Taylor," Chastity said. "Long time no hear."

"Chas, I need your help."

Fifteen minutes later, Taylor had a plan. She'd scheduled three different erotic acts for opening night, bumping up the heat level with each show. The first would be a role-play. Chastity assured her that "Sex with a Stranger" was their number one request. Next, a BDSM demo, and finally, a ménage.

If the shows sold out, she'd discuss future events with Jagger. *One step at a time.*

With the talent booked, she reserved one of the smaller ballrooms to hold the performances. Next, she brought her staff up to speed. These events were for guests who purchased a membership to the hotel's private club. Reservations were required, and every attendee must be carded before entering the salon.

Taylor sat with the hotel's Webmaster while she updated the Loving site. "Please include the words: 'Limited Availability' and 'Membership Required'," Taylor instructed. "And once we do that, let's highlight the segment of beach reserved for nude sunbathing."

Jagger's reputation was riding on this and she would treat these changes with the utmost care. With a relieved sigh, she returned to her office. *Now the hotel will sell out.*

After typing up a press release, she forwarded it to Jagger, and braced for the wrath of Kate. But the publicist didn't make an appearance all afternoon.

Jagger did.

Her heart skipped a beat. He walked into her office and shut the door. The air sizzled with excitement, their strong connection pulling her to her feet. She wanted to run to him and kiss him senseless.

"Hi," she said. "How'd your interviews go?"

"I have news." Brimming with confidence, and a smile that made her heart flutter, he rounded her desk and pulled her into his arms. "You were right." He kissed her before she could stop him, his mouth crushing her, his arms holding her flush against him.

She groaned into him and unleashed a kiss that said everything she could not. For once, she didn't even try to hold back.

"You feel incredible," he murmured. "Where did that come from?"

"You trusted me and I wanted to say thank you."

"I can't wait to see what you do after I tell you the latest."

She smiled. "Mr. Loving, why don't you have a seat?"

He leaned his butt on her desk and peered into her eyes. "In the past four hours, there's been a jump in bookings. We're at eighty-three percent and two of the three erotic events have already sold out." He grinned. "*You*. Are a genius."

With a prideful grin, she stroked his arm. Because she had to touch him. The zing of arousal traveled through her. "Congratulations."

"I wanted to take you out tonight, but Kate arranged a working dinner with area business execs and local politicos. She mentioned wanting to catch up with you, anyway."

"No time for that. I'm having a working dinner with my team. I want to add a spicy party into the mix for later in the week—

maybe a lingerie event—plus, I have a few other ideas I'll summarize in an email for your approval."

"You're on fire." He lifted her hand, kissed her finger. "Meet me at eleven, on the beach. I want to give you a proper thank you."

My ultimate fantasy. If she could find the courage to have sex on the beach, she would tell Jagger *exactly* how she felt about him. And she wouldn't hold back.

THE BEACH

As Taylor slipped outside, the cool night air whispered through her hair and she tugged her sweater shawl closer. A last-minute change of plans had Kate attending the business dinner with Jagger. And the anxiety about having to spend time with her former friend floated away as the excitement over seeing Jagger continued to build.

Now, as she hurried down the walkway, her insides hummed with excitement.

At the sidewalk's end, she slipped off her shoes and trudged forward in the cold sand. Her phone buzzed and she slowed to read the incoming text.

"Stay right there," Jagger texted.

From behind, strong hands wrapped her in a hug. "I've missed you." His familiar voice sent tingles skittering through her. "All I could think about tonight was you."

Her heart skipped a beat. Turning, she smiled. "Same here."

When he kissed her, she melted into him. "I have a surprise. You ready?"

She slipped her fingers through his and the warmth from his hand calmed her. "Lead the way."

They strolled down the stretch of dark beach, the lapping waves kissing the shoreline. After passing several large boulders, he stopped. "Our secret hideaway."

A large Mexican blanket had been spread over the sand and covered with beach towels. Faux pillar candles surrounded the romantic oasis, the flickering yellow light beckoning them over. A stack of folded blankets had been piled nearby. She spied two flutes and a bottle sticking out of a champagne bucket.

"Thank you," she murmured. "This is amazing."

As she sat, he lifted the bottle of sparkling water, opened it, and shot her a playful smile. "Hope you don't mind a twist-top," he said, and poured their drinks.

Laughing, she accepted the flute and he eased down next to her. "To you."

As they toasted, a gust of wind swirled her hair and she shivered. Jagger pulled a blanket off the pile, repositioned himself behind her, and cloaked them in a thick layer of warm cotton. She pulled up her knees and he tightened his hug. Together, they stared at the glittery moonlight dancing on the midnight ocean.

He nuzzled her neck, kissed her skin, then he lifted her onto his lap. "I want you, Taylor." With his arm draped around her shoulder, he kissed her. "I want to make your fantasy come true. Have sex on the beach with me."

Her breath hitched, her insides pulsed with arousal, and her heart leapt at the chance to be with this man again. Melissa's motto, "Life is all about making bold choices," had led her to this special moment...and to this amazing man.

But as she studied his handsome face, all the words about how she *really* felt got stuck in her throat. "I want you, too," was all she could murmur.

Slowly, they removed their clothing and snuggled beneath the blankets. Just being with Jagger was her ultimate fantasy. Soothed by the gentle ocean waves lapping the shore, she peered into his soulful eyes. His smile melted her. His kiss left her breathless. She tore open the condom packet, straddled him, and sheathed him. Rising up, she took him deep inside her, the ultimate pleasure streaking through her. Instead of moving, she peered down at him, eager to capture the memory of this wonderful man and this special moment.

His gaze roamed over her face and body. "You are so damned sexy."

Tears welled and she draped herself over him to conceal the unwelcomed emotion. He wrapped her in his strong arms and whispered, "Your beauty and strength are all I need."

Refusing to ruin the moment by crying, she began gliding on his shaft. The onslaught of euphoria stole her thoughts, and she got lost in everything Jagger.

She loved how his hands never stopped moving over her. How he shifted her so he could slip his hand between them and fondle her breasts, or how he caressed her bottom in a way that made her grind into him and growl with pleasure. But mostly, she just loved him.

"I'm going to…Oh, Jagger…" Her voice trailed off in a moan as the ecstasy overtook her. Convulsing and moaning through the orgasm, she couldn't mask the tears flowing down her cheeks. She wished she hadn't fallen so hard, so fast.

Still connected, he rolled them over. When he saw her dampened cheeks, his brow furrowed. "Happy tears, right?"

She smiled. "Very happy."

"We are good together," he said, before resuming his thrusting.

He held her like she was his. He kissed her like he couldn't live without her. The sexy sounds he made when he came inside her triggered another orgasm and she released a strangled cry as he poured himself into her.

In the aftermath, they snuggled close. She shouldn't be falling in love with him, but she was. Needing a moment to clear her head, she scooted out of his embrace.

"Be right back." Though chilled by the nighttime air, she

wrapped herself in another beach blanket, and hurried to the water's edge.

There, she turned her full attention toward the vastness of the star-filled sky, wishing on the brightest one for something that seemed absurd, even to her.

A moment later, he appeared next to her. "You have a thing about leaving me after loving me."

She glimpsed his naked body. "Do you want a blanket?"

"No, Taylor, I want you. I want you to stop being afraid of what's happening between us." He stood in front of her and laid strong hands on her shoulders. "Trust me."

"I do trust you, Jagger. It's myself I don't trust. I don't want to get hurt."

Pulling her into his arms, he kissed her forehead. "Come sit down. I have another surprise."

Once huddled beneath the blankets, he presented her with a small jewelry box. "I bought this at one of the boutique stores in the hotel. I wanted to get out, but the day—"

She pressed her fingers over his mouth. "You didn't have to buy me anything."

He shone his phone's flashlight onto the box. "Open it."

After lifting the lid, she gasped. "Jagger, it's beautiful." A striking sapphire bracelet laced with diamonds sparkled in the spotlight.

"The sapphires reminded me of your eyes, but no worries if you don't like it. You can exchange it for anything in any of the stores."

She melted. "I love it. I can't believe you did this."

He clasped the gift onto her wrist. She rose up on her knees and the blanket slipped off her shoulders. Pressing her hands to his face, she kissed him again and again. "Thank you. It's perfect and thoughtful and totally unexpected."

"You just described you. Happy Valentine's Day to my raven-haired beauty."

On a strangled sob, she threw her arms around him. Together, they fell backward onto the blanket. "Tell me you have more than that one condom," she said as tears streaked her cheeks.

"Bought a twelve-pack this time," he said, and they laughed.

They made love again. Though Taylor thought they should return to the hotel, Jagger asked her to fall asleep in his arms. She didn't want to leave him, so she stayed.

When she awoke, she checked the time on her phone. Just after four.

"Jagger, wake up. It's opening day and we have to get inside before the staff sees us."

"Get inside?" he asked. "If you say so."

He shot her a sleepy grin, kissed her cheek, and whispered, "Be my Valentine."

I love you. She couldn't say those words, so she settled for, "Only if you'll be mine."

Twenty minutes later, they rode the service elevator to the penthouse level. He stole one more kiss before she hurried down the hall, toward her suite.

When she entered, she expected silence and darkness. Instead, the room was ablaze with lights. Kate stopped pacing, crossed her arms, and scowled, as if Taylor had missed her curfew. Hoping to avoid a conversation, Taylor marched toward her bedroom.

"You had to go and ruin everything, didn't you?" Kate's staccato sliced through the cold silence.

"Stay out of my life," Taylor replied.

"Not when you're screwing my best client."

Taylor stopped and pivoted. With slow, deliberate steps, she walked toward Kate. In the past, Kate's death stare and intimidating nature had sent Taylor running scared. But not this time. "Back off, *Kathy.*"

"You're destroying Jagger's image—the image *I* restored. I do not want a repeat of last year. Jagger almost lost *everything* because he couldn't keep his dick in his pants. He was such a high-maintenance client I had to let everyone else go. It's taken me months to rebuild my client list. Jagger is one drink, one irrelevant fuck, one snort away from another catastrophic nosedive."

Taylor rolled her eyes. Nothing had changed. The earth still revolved around Kathy Jones. "Clearly, you don't know him."

"Jagger's going to break your heart," Kate continued. "I want to help ensure that doesn't happen. This time it's personal. We're friends."

"No," Taylor said, hitching her hands on her hips. "*Not* friends."

"You don't know this, dear, but wealthy playboys do whatever they want, whenever they want." Kate's syrupy voice grated on Taylor. "I'm going to be brutally honest. You're innocent and naïve. I'm worried that Jagger is using you, honey."

"You? Honest? When have you *ever* been honest?"

Kate's upper lip curled into a snarl.

"In tenth grade, I confided in you that I had a huge crush on Pete Strawbridge," Taylor began. "You told me you wanted to— and I quote—'help me get him'. A week later, you two were inseparable." She arched a brow. "Where I come from, that's *not* help."

Smirking, Kate shook her head. "C'mon, high school was a crazy time."

"We had round two in college," Taylor said. "This time, you helped yourself to Joe Greenway. Remember him? One minute he's my boyfriend, the next minute I found you with his dick in your mouth. But that's nothing compared to all the cheating you did every time we took a class together."

Kate's cheeks pinkened. "Me? Cheat? That's insane."

"You got called into the dean's office and somehow managed to talk your way out of that, too," Taylor said. "A few years ago, at a college reunion, I heard you paid a bunch of sorority sisters to ensure *you* got nominated for homecoming queen after you learned the sorority wanted *me* to represent them. That's classic Kathy. The day I cut ties with you was a good one."

Kate jabbed her index finger at Taylor. "When he starts screwing the masses, boozes it up...or worse, don't come crying to me."

"That's *your* baggage with Jagger, not mine." Taylor had had enough. She swiped her keycard, entered her bedroom, and kicked the door closed.

Shaking, Taylor crawled onto the bed and curled in a ball. Kathy Jones had succeeded in resurrecting old wounds and decade's worth of insecurities. Taylor shoved her face into the pillow and sobbed.

OPENING DAY, AND JAGGER was on top of the world. Loving Malibu was sold out. *She did it.* Surprised Taylor hadn't joined him for breakfast in the restaurant, he shot her a quick text. "Today will be mayhem. Thank you for everything."

But no dots appeared on the screen as he made his way toward his office.

Robby whirled in. "Congratulations, boss. This is a great day and I, for one, plan to enjoy every second of it. I hope you do, too. You deserve this success."

"I couldn't have gotten through the last two years without you. Thank you, Robby, for everything."

Robby cupped his hands over his heart. "You're going to make me cry."

"Cry *after* we get through today. Once guests start arriving and those champagne bottles are uncorked, things are going to get crazy."

. . .

THE DAY HAD BEEN a whirlwind of greeting guests, posing for photos, and talking with the press. And while the champagne flowed freely, Jagger didn't miss the bubbly. What he did miss was Taylor. He hadn't seen her all day.

Before the evening events got underway, he retreated to his suite. Several floral arrangements, and baskets filled with alcohol, adorned the living area. *I'll give the liquor to the staff tomorrow.* He dressed in his black tuxedo and simple black mask, the one he'd given Taylor to use. Missing the hell out of her, he called her.

"Hi," she answered.

Relieved to hear her voice, he smiled. "There you are. Can you stop by my suite?"

"Be there shortly."

Ten minutes later, there was a light tap on his door. Eager to see her, he flung it open. Her crimson halter evening gown hugged her curves; the matching masquerade mask made her blue eyes pop. "Wow, you look amazing." She'd pinned up her hair, reminding him of the night they'd met. "My raven-haired beauty."

But it was her confident smile that sent a burst of energy through him. After closing the door, he pulled her into his arms and inhaled everything Taylor. "I missed you today."

"Me, too. Did you see? All three shows are sold out."

He kissed her cheek. "My heroine."

"Hardly. You did this, Jagger. This is your win."

He dropped a light kiss on her lipstick-covered lips. "Come on in. I have something I've been meaning to give you."

Her face lit up. Holding her hand, he led her to the sofa. "Please, sit."

As her gaze swept over the wine and champagne baskets, her expression faltered.

"You're not worried I'm going to drink any of that, are you?"

For a brief second, concern laced her eyes. "No, of course not."

"Be right back." He retreated to his bedroom and grabbed the stilettos she'd left the night they'd met. Then, he knelt in front of her and swapped out her heels for those.

She couldn't mask the sadness in her eyes. "Thank you for returning my shoes."

Hoping to lighten the moment, he said, "It's more like 'If the shoes fit, you must be the girl of my dreams'."

"Aww, thank you." Her sweet smile slayed him, but he wasn't convinced she was okay.

"Ready to head downstairs?" he asked, pushing off the floor.

As she rose, she grabbed the discarded shoes and hurried toward the door. "I'll drop these in my suite and see you there."

Taylor's jitters worried him. Something was definitely wrong. Three easy strides and he stood beside her. "You're not okay. Talk to me." Hoping to comfort her, he ran a hand over her shoulder. Instead of relaxing, she stiffened.

"I'm sorry. I'm fine. It's been a long day. Of course I'll join you."

He couldn't fathom what had caused the abrupt change, but he was late to his own event. The masquerade party was well underway and he was slated to address the guests fifteen minutes ago. "I'm giving a brief speech in the ballroom. Join me."

"I've got to check on the performers." She opened the door and stepped into the hallway.

"You'll have time. You're part of my leadership team and I want you onstage with me."

After dropping off her shoes, they waited for the elevator in a chilly silence. The doors slid open and, as they squeezed inside, Jagger greeted his guests with a smile. "How's everyone doing?"

"Having a great time!" one guest replied.

"Can't wait for the sexy show," answered another.

"Loved my spa day," replied a third.

He knew Taylor well enough to see past her polite smile, but he'd no idea what had triggered her walled-off attitude. Everyone piled out on the first floor. As they approached the ballroom, the pulsing beat of the band pounded in his chest. No sooner had they stepped inside than several VIP guests ambushed him.

Taylor kept her distance. But he wanted her flush against him. *Goddammit, she's mine and I want the world to know.* With a firm hand on her elbow, he guided her toward the front of the room.

The band finished their number and Jagger took center stage. With mic in hand, he smiled at the masked crowd. "Good evening and welcome to Loving Malibu." After the applause died down, he continued. "Is everyone having a good time?"

He paused to appreciate the crowd's shouts and cheers. During his lowest point, he doubted this moment would ever happen.

"I have a phenomenal team I'd like you to meet," he continued. "They're the real reason you're having a great time." As he introduced his executive team, they lined up behind him.

"Robby, c'mon up here." His very smiley assistant hopped onstage and stood beside him. "If you don't have an excellent assistant, I highly recommend you get one. Robby Sutton is indispensible." Robby beamed as Jagger touted how invaluable he was to the success of Loving. When finished, Robby took a melodramatic bow, and the audience burst into applause.

"If you attended an event, or if you're going to attend one later this evening, you might want to personally thank my event director, Taylor Hathaway."

She walked onstage, stood beside Jagger, and smiled at the guests.

"Taylor Hathaway is my lucky charm," Jagger continued. "Her efforts, and those of her team, should be hailed as heroic." He paused while the audience applauded. "They worked nonstop to ensure a variety of activities. There's something fun for everyone. Parasailing and wine tours. Who's signed up for Chess on the Beach tomorrow?" With a smile, he nodded as several raised their hands. "That event is sold out for days. And we've got some sexy shows that will get your blood-a-pumpin'." The crowd laughed. "Be sure to thank her when you see her."

Her large, blue eyes blinked away the moisture. "Thank you," she whispered.

She wasn't anywhere near ready to hear what he wanted to tell her, but there was no way he could live without her. No fucking way.

After more applause, Jagger said, "Thank you for making Loving Malibu the place to be. Have a great evening and a fantastic stay." He handed the mic to the band's lead singer and gestured for his team to file off the stage.

"Thank you for the public recognition," Taylor said. "I'm going to make sure the salon is all set and check on the performers."

Needing answers, he said, "I'll join you."

As they made their way through the mingling guests, Kate bustled over. "Very nice speech. Some VIP's are requesting face time with the master of ceremonies." She shot Taylor a quick smile. "I'm so sorry to break you two up."

"I'll catch up with you as soon as I can," Jagger said to Taylor.

Before opening the door to the ballroom, she glanced over her shoulder at him. His chest tightened. Something was definitely wrong. *Dammit, is she going to bolt on me...again?*

11

THE EMERGENCY ROOM

Taylor hurried down the hallway, pausing briefly at the registration table to speak with David and Adele before entering the empty salon. Grateful for a moment alone, she crumpled into a chair near the back of the quiet room.

Her temporary assignment at Loving was ending. Tomorrow. And her heart was breaking. She'd been elated when Jagger had invited her into his suite because she'd assumed he was going to offer her the position, or tell her he didn't want her to leave. When he'd gotten down on one knee, she'd almost burst into tears. Instead, he'd given her back her shoes. Leaping to *that* conclusion had been humiliating and she couldn't get away from him fast enough.

In a short amount of time, they'd forged a special bond. She shouldn't have fantasized about being with him long-term, but she had. By doing that, she'd set herself up for heartache. As she glanced down, the sparkle from the bracelet caught her eye. *Stop being selfish. This is Jagger's big day and all I can think about is myself. I'm no better than Kate and I owe him an apology.*

Steeling her spine, she shifted her thoughts to the task at hand. Her job at Loving wasn't over *yet* and she owed him her utmost professionalism. The upcoming shows were the pinnacle of the resort's grand opening. And she was committed to ensuring each went off without a hitch. Which meant, she'd stay and watch, no matter how uncomfortable she felt.

"Excuse me," said someone behind her.

Rising, Taylor approached a man wearing a suit, but no mask. "Are you here for the show?"

"Taylor, I'm Dusty Whitner of Whitner Hospitality. I'm very impressed with what you've done for Loving Resorts and I'd like to discuss the possibility of your working for me."

JAGGER NEEDED TO FIND Taylor. The forty minutes he spent with his VIP guests was more than enough. Not even Kate's evil eye could stop him. As he headed toward the salon, his phone rang.

"Loving."

"Sir, it's Enrique." His concierge.

"Everything okay?"

"Robby was taken away in an ambulance."

"Call for a car. I'll be there shortly." Jagger hung up and peered down the hallway. David and Adele sat behind a registration table outside the salon. Rather than alarm the staff, he texted Taylor.

"Robby taken to ER by ambulance. No idea why. Headed there now. Keep this to yourself. Sorry to miss the erotic show with you." He slipped his phone into his pocket and powered toward the lobby.

Stopping in front of the concierge's desk, he removed his mask. "What happened?"

"I don't know," Enrique said, "but he was taken out on a stretcher. Harbor-UCLA Medical Center."

Forty-five long minutes later, Jagger charged into the emergency room. After he spoke with the receptionist, she buzzed him through the double doors to triage. He found Robby resting, his red eyes swollen closed and his skin covered in giant red splotches.

Robby tilted his head back to see. "What are you doing here?"

"Jesus, what happened?" Jagger asked, dragging a chair over.

"I told them not to tell you." Pausing, Robby sipped from a Styrofoam cup. "I had an allergic reaction, but I'm okay."

Robby didn't just have allergic reactions. He had anaphylactic ones. "What did you eat?"

"Food. Delicious, yummy food."

"Robby, this is serious. You scared the hell out of me."

"I ate whatever Kate gave me."

"*What?* Did you check with her?"

"Of course I did. She told me there was no shellfish."

Jagger called his chef and hit the speaker button. "Charles, it's Jagger. Robby had a serious allergic reaction. I'm with him in the ER."

"Hi, Charles," Robby said.

"Oh, no, I'm sorry to hear that," Charles said. "Remind me what you're allergic to again."

"Shellfish and peanut butter."

"Did you dine in the restaurant?" Charles asked.

"No. Since I hadn't eaten all day, Kate brought me a plate of hors d'oeuvres."

"With so many food restrictions, I made hors d'oeuvres to suit every palate," the chef said. "Everything was carefully labeled with tent cards. Where's my list? Ah, here it is. There was seafood in the lobster muffins with poached egg, caviar, spinach and hollandaise. Shrimp drizzled with peanut sauce. And deviled eggs with langoustine lobster tails. I'm sorry, Robby, and I hope you're okay. The restaurant is packed. I've got to run."

"Thanks for taking my call." Jagger hung up.

"I didn't eat shrimp," Robby said, "but I wouldn't have eaten the muffins or the deviled eggs if I'd known they were made with lobster."

"Does Kate know about your allergy?" Jagger asked.

"Awhile back we talked about food allergies. Her husband has the exact opposite allergy as me. He's allergic to fish, like tuna and salmon, but not shellfish." He set down the cup. "Anyway, I'm stable and the itching has subsided. It was an accident."

Jagger's stomach clenched. *I'm not so sure about that.*

TAYLOR CHATTED BRIEFLY WITH the hotel owner. She didn't want to be rude, but she had no interest in working for Whitner Hospitality. Once he left, she confirmed the first two erotic performers were ready, and checked in with the audio engineer. Since the talent couldn't wear mics, stage props had to be wired for sound. Once her checklist had been completed, she left the salon to speak with David and Adele.

"You guys look great," Taylor said. "Love that mask, Adele."

"The feathers are driving me nuts," David said. "They keep getting in my mouth."

With an eye roll, Adele rose. "Trade seats with me."

Taylor waited while they switched places. "Have either of you seen Jagger? He's speaking to the audience before the show starts."

"Nope," David replied, adjusting his mask.

"Some time ago, I saw him heading this way," Adele replied. "But he got a call and flipped back toward the lobby."

Furrowing her brow, Taylor glanced down the hallway. "Hmm, I wonder what that was about."

"Text him," David said.

"I left my phone in my room, charging," Taylor said.

"Use mine." David lifted his from the inside pocket of his tuxedo and tapped the home key. "Oops, it's dead."

Adele checked in several guests and David jumped up to open the salon door.

"You're going to have to introduce the first couple," Adele said as a line formed at the registration table.

Again, Taylor glanced down the hall, hoping to see Jagger. Unless he showed up in the next five minutes, she'd have to do it.

As guests took their seats, Taylor waited in the wings, mic in hand. Butterflies fluttered in her stomach. *I did this once. I can do it again.*

When David closed the salon doors, Taylor walked onstage as the audio engineer started the smooth jazz music.

Be bold. Surveying the packed room, she smiled. "Good evening, I'm Taylor Hathaway, event director. Welcome to the spicier side of Loving. Before we get started, I'd like to remind you that these taboo relationships will be performed by professional sex artists. So, when *inspiration* strikes you"—she paused while the audience laughed—"please play in your suite. If you get rambunctious in your seats, security will remove you. Let's not upstage the performers. They work *hard* for you."

She waited while the audience applauded.

"Time to turn up the heat. Though strangers, our first couple doesn't stay that way for long. Ladies and gentlemen, 'The Massage'."

Taylor walked off the stage and up the aisle so she could watch from the back of the room.

An attractive man, wearing a fluffy white robe, walked onstage and disrobed, revealing his muscular, naked form. He slipped beneath the linens on the massage table and lay on his back. A flashy woman sauntered over, dressed in a short, black, front-zipper dress that displayed her ample cleavage. Her patent leather thigh-high boots glistened beneath the lights. As they exchanged pleasantries, she uncovered his shoulders, slicked her hands in oil, and began massaging.

"How's my pressure?" she asked, stroking his skin.

"The harder, the better."

She peeled back the sheet so she could massage his chest. "Your muscles are super tense."

"Mmm, that feels great," he said.

As she leaned over him, her breasts spilled from the dress. "What about this? Is this okay?"

"Definitely."

"If you're interested, I offer a different type of massage."

"How so?"

"I *start* with a happy ending so you can be more relaxed for the rest of the massage."

"Baby, that sounds perfect."

She massaged his groin over the linens until his cock tented the sheet. "Feels fantastic," he said, and released a long, deep groan.

She pulled a foil packet from her pocket, slowly unzipped her dress, and let the garment drop to the floor.

"Wow," he said, eyeing her naked body.

After tossing off the blanket, she mounted him, and rolled the condom over his jutting erection. Then, she coated her hands in more lubricant and massaged his cock. Up and down with slow, tantalizing strokes. With a gleam in her eyes, she placed him at her opening and took him inside.

The audience's collective moan filled the otherwise hushed room.

Gliding on her client's shaft, the masseuse arched her back and fondled her breasts until they shimmered beneath the stage lights.

So much had changed since the last time Taylor had seen this type of show. Rather than blushing and cringing, she stood with confidence. The woman's dirty talk, paired with the man's grunts and groans, made her insides throb, but she ached for the one man who could bring her relief and fill her soul with love.

Despite feeling heartbroken about leaving, she was returning home with a newfound confidence. That would never have happened if she hadn't worked for Jagger. By helping him overcome his issues, she'd been forced to confront hers.

As the couple neared their climactic ending, several in the audience fidgeted in their chairs, while one man hurried from the salon.

Taylor slipped out and over to the registration table, still being manned by Adele and David. The thirty-minute break between shows would allow time to grab her phone and text Jagger. Was he purposefully avoiding the entertainment or had something else detained him?

"Adele, can you cover for me?" Taylor asked. "I'll be back before the next show begins."

After Adele agreed, Taylor headed toward the elevators. Once on her floor, she walked down the quiet hall and into her suite.

Kate, dressed in a gown, sat sobbing on the sofa, a tablet on her lap. "What's wrong?" Taylor asked as she removed her masquerade mask.

Black trails of mascara streaked down Kate's cheeks and her nose glowed bright red. "I am ruined. He's ruined. You want to know why bringing back the smut was a terrible idea?" On a loud sniffle, she shoved the tablet at Taylor. "Here's your answer!"

As soon as Taylor glimpsed the photo, her stomach dropped. Jagger was sitting in bed with a woman, her nude back to the camera. "Where did you get this?"

"A reporter staying in the hotel." Kate started sobbing again. "He's trashed out of his mind and I blame you."

"Ohmygod," Taylor whispered. She pressed her hand over her heart to soothe the shooting pain. Had she done this? Was she to blame for Jagger's setback?

"There's more than one photo," Kate croaked out.

Taylor swiped the screen. Jagger was in bed with two women. *Ohgod, no.* She swiped the screen again. He was kissing the first, while the second snapped a shot of her breasts pressed against his face. *Something isn't right.* Taylor swiped back to the first photo and enlarged it.

In addition to Jagger's hair being shorter, he had a dime-sized mole on his upper chest, near his shoulder. Either this photo had been doctored, or it had been taken a while ago, because he had no distinguishing mark like that on his chest or anywhere else. And she ought to know. She'd stared at his gorgeous, naked body like an artist studies his nude model.

Until she could figure out what Kate was up to, she'd say nothing. Despite not knowing where Jagger was, she refused to believe he was drunk and screwing two women. The one thing Kate could count on was Taylor running scared. *Not this time.*

"Why show these to me? Shouldn't you be corralling your drunk client back into his pen?"

"I told you if you flaunted tits and ass, he'd get caught up in it," Kate said, her voice thick with smugness. "I warned you, but you wouldn't listen to me."

"The hotel is sold out." Taylor hitched her hands on her hips. "Jagger wanted results and he got them, plain and simple."

"I'm going to start damage control, and I'd hate to have to rake your good name through the muck. The shit is going to get so deep, I'm not sure I can pull poor Jagger out this time." Glaring at her, Kate rose. "If I were you, I'd be on the next plane back east."

"If you were me, you wouldn't be such a bitch." Taylor tossed the tablet on the sofa, and walked away. After shutting her bedroom door, a little smile danced on the corners of her lips. *I'm not going anywhere.*

Hoping Jagger had contacted her, she grabbed her phone. And her mouth fell open as she read the waiting texts.

"Robby taken to ER by ambulance," texted Jagger. "No idea why. Headed there now. Keep this to yourself. Sorry to miss the erotic show with you."

Fifty minutes after the first text, he'd sent another. "Anaphylactic reaction. Doc stabilized him. Everything OK?"

Oh, no. Poor Robby. "Didn't have phone until now," she texted. "Sorry to hear about Robby. Everything's going great. ETA?"

Tiny dots appeared, and then his text. "Waiting to see if they're keeping him overnight or discharging. I'll text you when I know more. How was the first show?"

"Sexy. Heading back for the second. Tell Robby I hope he's OK."

More tiny dots and then a red heart appeared. She replied with an X and an O.

Before leaving her bedroom, she viewed herself in the mirror. "I'm good just the way I am." Though she didn't fully believe herself, she smiled at her reflection. She was moving in the right direction, one step at a time.

12

THE TRUTH

I T WAS PAST THREE in the morning when Jagger returned to the hotel. After getting Robby settled, he strode through the quiet lobby toward the back of the property. Once outside, he hurried down the beach, quickly passing the boulders.

Taylor was staring at the ocean, wrapped in a blanket, and surrounded by faux candles. His heart beat faster. He loved her so much, and for so many reasons.

Sinking down, he greeted her with a kiss. "Hello, beautiful."

Her smile set his heart afire and the happiness in her eyes settled his soul. He framed her face with his hands and dropped several worshipful kisses on her mouth. "Your lips are cold. Have you been outside long?"

She draped a blanket around his back and he pulled her flush against him. "Long enough to calm down. Before we get into all of that, I owe you an apology."

"For what?" he asked, furrowing his brow.

"I got weird when you gave me back my shoes and I'm very sorry."

His eyes softened. "It's okay."

She kissed his cheek. "Thank you. So, what happened to Robby? Is he okay?"

"Kate gave him shellfish. I hate to think she did that on purpose."

"I wouldn't put it past her." Breaking eye contact, Taylor shifted her sights toward the never-ending ocean. "That's not all she's done."

After she explained how Kate had attempted to sabotage their relationship, Jagger's eyes grew cold. "She sickens me. How'd you know those were old photos?"

"Your hair was shorter and I noticed a mole on your chest that's not there now."

"Nice catch. I had a precancerous growth removed." He shifted his sights toward the shoreline. "I'm sorry you had to see those pictures. That was me hitting rock bottom."

She rose on her knees and faced him. "*Was*, as in, past tense."

Her sweet expression grounded him. "Your trust means everything to me." Before she could reply, he stole another kiss. "I thought you and Kate were old friends."

"Total frenemies." She shivered. "She was counting on my running scared. But you changed me, Jagger."

"No, babe. *You* changed you," Jagger said before cloaking her in a blanket. "All I did was help you realize the truth."

"I want to tell you something," she whispered. "It sounds stupid when compared with your—"

"Taylor." He cupped her chin. "No comparing."

"Okay." She cleared her throat. "I was a skinny kid. Super skinny. Dorky and uncoordinated, too. I was always the last one to get picked for a team sport. Mean girls poked fun at me. *A lot.* In high school, several boys commented on my flat chest."

He grimaced. "That's harsh. They'd regret their words if they saw you now."

"Thank you," she said. "Seeing Kate stirred up my insecurities.

But I'm determined to move beyond them and accept myself the way I am."

Her inner strength tugged at his heart. But his happiness was overshadowed by the damage Kate had caused. She had to be dealt with. Anger clouded his thoughts and he shoved off the ground. "I'm going to fire her, but not before I talk to Robby about pressing charges."

"All of that can wait." Taylor patted the empty spot. "C'mon back down here and stay with me awhile." Her voice turned playful. "Time for a *massage*. I picked up some pointers earlier and want to try them out."

She's right. He exhaled a huff as he eased back down and scooped her onto his lap. With a lighthearted laugh, she wrapped her arms around his neck. For now, he'd focus on what really mattered. And that was Taylor.

"Good show?" he asked.

"I'll reenact it and let you decide."

"I already know I'm going to love it." He tightened his hold. "Thank you for insisting I add the kink."

"It was my pleasure," she said, combing her fingers through his hair. Though she smiled, sadness banked in her eyes.

And he knew why. While at the hospital, Robby had mentioned she'd booked her return flight the following day because her boss expected her back at work. Jagger suspected her hasty departure had nothing to do with Colton and everything to do with him. For the moment, he'd say nothing. He had loose ends to tie up, a publicist to fire, and one hell of a surprise to prepare for.

"I missed you, tonight," he murmured, nibbling her earlobe. When his mouth found hers, her soft moans and tender touch turned him hard. But being with her revolved around much more than coupling. Their relationship was grounded in trust and in facing fears. They believed in each other and, in turn, themselves.

In Taylor, he'd found a home that none of his hotels could ever give him.

The kiss ended and she hugged him. Her sweet essence surrounded him, confirming what he already knew. She was the one.

"Tonight, I want to watch us in the mirror...one more..." Her voice cracked and she bowed her head. Allowing her a moment, he dropped a kiss on her forehead. "Without a mask," she continued. "Not just for you, but for me, too."

"My brave, raven-haired beauty." They lay beneath the blankets and snuggled close. He wanted her to know how he felt, before she left. "I love you," he whispered as they gazed up at the bejeweled night sky.

Lifting her face, she peered into his eyes. "I love you, too, Jagger."

Their tender kisses and soft giggles bowed to heart-filled passion. Jagger made love to her like it was their last time.

Because if she wasn't willing to uproot her life, it very well could be.

13

THE HARDEST GOODBYE

FIGHTING BACK TEARS, TAYLOR buckled her seatbelt and shifted her attention out the aircraft window.

She and Jagger had said their goodbyes at six that morning. He hadn't asked her to stay. He hadn't offered her a job. He'd walked her to her suite, wished her a safe flight, and left.

And that's when her heart had shattered.

With her assignment completed, she'd head home rather than tack on the time off Colton had offered. If she vacationed alone, she'd mope all week. It would be smarter to immerse herself in everything Mitus and move on.

She fiddled with the sapphire and diamond bracelet dangling from her wrist. It was a bittersweet reminder she'd tuck away in her jewelry box once she returned home. *Love just wasn't enough.*

Passengers traipsed down the aisle on their way to business class, but her companion seat in first class remained empty. Fishing her phone from her handbag, she activated "airplane mode" and tossed her things onto the empty seat. When she closed her eyes, Jagger's chiseled face popped into her head. If she lived to be a hundred, she'd never get over him. His easygoing smile was etched into her soul. And that mouth...the way he kissed her, held her. *I'm a mess.*

To distract herself, she watched baggage handlers hoist luggage onto the conveyor belt. Again, her thoughts drifted back to him.

Jagger had helped her take the first step in conquering lifelong insecurities. And for that, she'd always be grateful.

She loved working with him and helping him overcome his own challenges. Her chest tightened. *We made a great team.*

"Excuse me." She whipped her head toward the familiar voice, and her heart leapt into her throat. "Your handbag is in my seat." With a wicked grin, Jagger offered it to her.

She absentmindedly took it, disbelieving he was actually standing there.

"Hello, beautiful." He leaned over and kissed her cheek before sitting. "You didn't think I was going to let you return to Virginia without me, did you?"

"I...I did." She stroked his arm. Had to confirm he was really there.

Shaking his head, his sexy smile said it all. "Not a chance. When you know, you know."

Her heart skipped a beat and she flashed him a grin. "How long will you be staying?"

"Long enough for you to resign and pack your bags."

She gaped at him. "Did you just offer me a job?"

"Yes, and I'm about to offer you a hell of a lot more than that." He pulled something from his jacket pocket, knelt in the aisle, and opened a ring box. "I love you. So damned much. I can't live without you and I don't want to run Loving without you by my side. Please marry me, Taylor."

"Ohmygod," she whispered.

In mid-sentence, the flight attendant stopped instructing passengers on safety precautions. "Ladies and gentleman, we have a proposal."

The cabin grew quiet. Taylor's heart pounded a frenzied rhythm, the excitement threatening to explode. "Yes, I will. Absolutely, *yes!*"

Passengers seated nearby clapped. He kissed her again before slipping the diamond on her finger. "I will cherish you for the rest of my life," he whispered.

With a triumphant smile, he rose and gave the thumbs-up sign. "She said 'Yes'!"

The cabin erupted in applause as he took his seat and the flight attendant resumed her preflight instructions.

He cupped her face, pulled her close, and kissed her again. "I love you so much. Will you be my forever Valentine?"

"I love you, too," she said, tears spilling from her. "You've made me so happy." She pressed her hand to her chest and sucked in a jagged breath.

"Me, too."

As the plane taxied toward the runway, she admired her diamond. "This is gorgeous."

"That ring is a placeholder, honey. We're going ring shopping."

She loved how the double halo of sparkling, round diamonds complemented the brilliance of the large solitaire. "Did you pick this out?"

"Yes, but it's from my hotel, Taylor."

"Even better," she said, weaving her fingers through his. "I love *this* ring that *you* picked out at *your* hotel. It's perfect."

He leaned close. "Do you know how happy I am that you said 'Yes'?"

"Yeah, I think I do," she said and kissed him. "So, about that job...are you offering me the position of Event Director at Loving Malibu?"

"Hell, no, that's not nearly big enough for someone with your skills, intelligence, and determination. I'm thinking more like Vice President of Events for Loving Resorts, worldwide."

"*What?* You can't be serious?" she asked as the plane sped down the runway and lifted into the sky.

"Of course I am. I need your loving touch at all my properties, so I'm creating this position just for you. Plus, I have plans for a fifth in Marco Island that we can develop *together* from the ground up."

"I would love that." Her gleeful expression faltered and she broke eye contact.

"What's wrong?"

"I'm going to miss everyone at Mitus."

"Take some time to decide. It's a lot to digest."

Bold choices. "No time needed. I'm following my heart. And my heart is with you. And... I've gotta admit, this is a great career move for me."

He chuffed out a laugh. "For us both."

The flight attendant appeared with two mini champagne bottles and two flutes perched on a tray. "On behalf of the captain and flight crew, congratulations on your engagement."

"Thank you," Taylor said. "That's so nice of you, but we don't drink. Do you have sparkling water?"

"Be right back with that." The flight attendant retreated to the front of the cabin.

"You don't have to stop drinking because of me," he said.

"I might have a glass of wine on occasion, but I want to support you in your sobriety."

His eyes softened. "You're an angel, you know that?"

She leaned close, kissed him. "There *is* something I'd love to do and you're the perfect man for the job."

"Name it."

Pressing her mouth to his ear, she whispered, "Become a member of the 'Mile High Club'."

His breathing hitched. "Aren't you a naughty girl?"

With a smirk, she nodded.

"I'm not a member of that club, either," he murmured. "But I don't have any condoms with me."

"I can wait until the return flight," she said, and squeezed his hand.

His loving kiss melted her heart and lit her insides on fire. "So can I, my love. So can I."

A NOTE FROM STONI

Thank you so much for reading THE LOVING TOUCH! Sign up for my newsletter on my website and I'll gift you a free steamy short story, only available to my Inner Circle.

Here's where you can follow me online. I look forward to connecting with you!

StoniAlexander.com
Amazon
BookBub
Facebook
Goodreads

Want to read more in The Touch Series? Here's Book Four...

THE HOTT TOUCH
BOOK FOUR OF THE TOUCH SERIES

Everyone adores ex-SEAL Maverick Hott, especially the ladies. That's the way it's always been. But he keeps things casual, so no one captures his heart. And no one gets hurt.

Most of all, him.

Then, there's beautiful Carly Stone. His bestie since they were kids. The girl who breathed life back into him when tragedy struck. The same one who runs him ragged on the racquetball court and sees into his soul with those piercing hazel eyes.

Yeah, *that* best friend.

Returning home after a near fatal hostage rescue mission, the fearless and cocky CEO of ThunderStrike has a brand new set of priorities...starting with her. But he stumbles upon her secret, which has him questioning how well he really knows her.

When a powerful senator calls in a favor and Maverick refuses, the ruthless politico exacts his revenge. So Maverick turns to the person he trusts most.

Carly's investigative skills are an asset. Her assets, a major distraction. And while posing as husband and wife, their chemistry is downright lethal.

Together, they're unstoppable...until Carly gets caught in the crosshairs, and the most important mission of Maverick's life is saving hers.

Grab THE HOTT TOUCH or Read FREE on Kindle Unlimited!

READ THE ENTIRE TOUCH SERIES
BY STONI ALEXANDER

LOOKING FOR A SEXY STANDALONE?
Check out BEAUTIFUL STEPBROTHER,
also by Stoni Alexander

Buy BEAUTIFUL STEPBROTHER or Read FREE on Kindle
Unlimited!

ACKNOWLEDGEMENTS

I am forever grateful to my husband, Johnny, for that life-changing conversation. I create heroes, but you are my real-life one. Thank you for your smarts, patience, and ability to keep me laughing all these years. Being easy on the eyes doesn't hurt either.

My son is my greatest inspiration. I pray and hope and wish that you achieve your goals and dreams as you take that next step in life. Thank you for being such a blessing in mine. You still make me laugh harder than anyone...even more than Dad.

Simply stated, my editor is the absolute best. Nicole, you are *indispensable*.

Carole, you truly are too thorough for words and a trusted ally. Thank you for your eagle eye and for loving all of my stories.

Thank you to my ever-talented critique group who doesn't love all my words, but finds loving ways to tell me. Magda, MC, and Andy: I value your input and appreciate your efforts.

I am grateful and humbled by the hard-working bloggers and reviewers who take the time to read and review my novels. Thank you, thank you for sharing my stories with your followers!

A special shout-out to India, Emma, Beca, Amanda, Judy, Crystal, and Mary for your reviews of WILDE. You lovely ladies blow me away with your kindness and support. Thank you for *getting* me and my stories, and for shouting it from the rooftops!

And, finally, for every woman who doesn't like what she sees in the mirror. I understand. You are not alone. Please know that you are beautiful, unique, and here on planet earth for a reason. We come in different shapes, sizes, and colors...united by our universal ability to love.

ABOUT THE AUTHOR

Stoni Alexander writes sexy romantic suspense and contemporary romance about tortured alpha males and independent, strong-willed females. Her passion is creating love stories where the hero and heroine help each other through a crisis so that, in the end, they're equal partners in more ways than love alone.

In a previous life, she appeared in numerous television, film and stage productions before transitioning to a successful career in business. Stoni spent her childhood moving around the country and appreciates her deep-seated roots in the DC Metro area. She's married to the love of her life, is an über-proud football mom, and dreams of the day when her muse will inspire her at will.

Made in the USA
Middletown, DE
11 July 2021